The Vampi

"Count Alucard!" cried l... which stretched before him. He had intended to call out loudly and clearly but the sound that had come out of his mouth was a croaking hiss. Henry Hollins cleared his throat and tried again. "Count Alucard! It's *me*! Henry Hollins!" He paused, and listened hard, but there was nothing to be heard. "There's nothing to be afraid of, Count! Surely you remember me? I came to your castle in Transylvania. Henry Hollins! I'm your *friend!*"

by the same author

THE
VAMPIRE'S
HOLIDAY

Willis Hall

Illustrated by Babette Cole

RED FOX

A Red Fox Book

Published by Random House Children's Books
20 Vauxhall Bridge Road, London SW1V 2SA

A division of Random House UK Ltd
London Melbourne Sydney Auckland
Johannesburg and agencies throughout the world

First published by The Bodley Head Children's Books 1992

Red Fox edition 1994

3 5 7 9 10 8 6 4

Printed and bound in Great Britain by
The Guernsey Press Co Ltd, Vale, Guernsey, C.I.

RANDOM HOUSE UK Limited Reg. No. 954009

Papers used by Random House UK Limited
are natural, recyclable products made from wood
grown in sustainable forests. The manufacturing processes
conform to the environmental regulations
of the country of origin.

ISBN 0 09 929321 8

Dedicated to my son James

"*Sacré bleu!*" muttered Captain André Amiens, as he spat the blackened stub of a well-chewed cigar out of his mouth and ground it on to the floor of the wheelhouse with the heel of his boot. "Did you ever see such weather?" he continued to the ginger-bearded man at his side. "Where has it come from?"

The tiny, paint-peeled Belgian cargo boat, *La Bernache*, slapped her bows into the teeth of the howling gale which raged along the length of the east coast of England. Driving rain lashed the wheelhouse and the automatic wiper on the window coughed and spluttered, unused to dealing with such frenzied weather.

"Hoots, mon! I'll tell ye where it's come frae!" growled Hamish McWhister, the Glasgow-born mate, nodding down towards the ship's prow where a length of black plastic sheeting, tightly lashed to the deck, concealed a rectangular item of the ship's cargo. "Did I nae tell ye to expect trouble, when you agreed to ferry yon diabolical article across the Channel? If ye had one ounce of sense in y'r body, ye'd ditch it over the side this minute!"

Captain Amiens frowned, but made no immediate reply. His lips were clamped together as, with both hands clenched on the ship's wheel, he strove against the gale to keep his vessel from overturning in the storm-tossed waters of the night. "Hold your tongue!" snarled the Belgian ship's master, finding his own tongue at last. "I promised to deliver that packing-case safely into Whitby harbour, and I mean to do so."

"Packing-case? Packing-case!" echoed the bearded Scot. "Will ye no stop calling it a packing-case, and tell it the way it is, mon! Stop your shilly-shallying! It's a coffin. You know it's a coffin. I know it's a coffin. Aye, and we both ken full well whose coffin it is, too! Why, if the crew should ever get to know the awful nature of what lies beneath that sheeting—"

"But the crew do not know, M'sieur McWhister!" Amiens broke in, his dark eyes flashing angrily as he glowered into the Scotsman's craggy face. "And they will never find out! You agreed to keep your silence on that account when the cargo came aboard at Le Havre. You're being paid well enough."

Hamish McWhister nodded gloomily, as he stared out at the foaming sea and the dark, starless night. "Aye, that's true," he answered with a sigh. "But I wish I had'nae ever set eyes on the money." He took hold of the brass handrail as the wheel-house deck pitched violently beneath his feet. "It's the devil's work we've taken on for ourselves this night."

The gale was buffeting against the side of *La Bernache*, forcing the little vessel to keel over into the pitching sea which crashed over the bulwark and pounded along the length of the deck. A bolt of lightning lit up the entire ship and, for a split second, joined sea and sky together.

"Mark my words, skipper," added McWhister, ominously, "it's the devil we'll have to answer to, as well, before this night is out."

Again, the Belgian captain made no reply. His duel with the storm was again demanding all his concentration.

"My goodness me, Albert!" said Emily Hollins, peering out of the window of their holiday caravan. "If I'd known before we left home that there'd be this kind of weather, I wouldn't have bothered to set off in the first place, if you want my—" Emily broke off, almost losing her footing, as the caravan shook to its foundations in the high wind. "Are you quite sure it's safe?" she continued, nervously. "We aren't going to go rolling off across the park and over the cliff?"

"I hardly think that's on the cards, Emily," observed her husband, Albert, winking across the Monopoly board at their eleven-year-old son, Henry. "We're not on wheels, you know."

"Aren't we?" asked Emily. "That's news to me. I thought all caravans were on wheels – that's how you can tell they're caravans."

"Hey up!" said Albert Hollins, raising his eyebrows with delight as he scanned the wording on the "Community Chest" card he had just picked up. "I've won Second Prize in a Beauty Contest. Pass me a tenner out of the bank, Henry." Then, as Henry counted out the money, Albert continued to Emily: "They're not *just* caravans, these aren't, Emily. They're holiday *homes*. They're static. They've had their wheels taken off."

Earlier that year, the Hollins family had decided to do something different for their annual holiday and, after a great deal of discussion, and much thumbing through of travel agents' brochures, they had plumped for three weeks at the Scarcombe Caravan Leisure Park, on Yorkshire's east coast. "That'll suit me down to the ground!" Albert had announced, when he read that the camp boasted both a nine-hole golf course *and* a bowling green. "That's just what the doctor ordered!" Emily had agreed, when she heard that there were an on-site restaurant/take-away, a launderette and a hair salon. Henry, who'd said nothing at all, was enthusiastic at the idea of spending a few weeks in a caravan – with or without wheels.

Now Emily's hopes of an idyllic holiday were fading fast as she gazed glumly at the rain-washed window and listened to the wind which had been howling outside the caravan since the moment they arrived that afternoon.

"What are we going to *do* tomorrow, if this keeps up?" she asked.

"Hey up – Fenchurch Street Station! I own

that!" said Albert, as Henry moved his galleon-piece round the board. "That's twenty-five pounds you owe me. Cough up." Then, in answer to Emily's question, he continued: "We've got plenty to do. We've got Monopoly, we've got Cluedo, we've got Scrabble. What about this for an idea: if it's still chucking it down at lunch-time tomorrow, we'll have a game of Scrabble and whoever loses gets into their wellies and nips across to the take-away for three cheeseburgers and chips."

Emily pulled a face. The idea of playing board games all through the holiday did not appeal to her one little bit. For one thing, she was hoping to pop into Scarcombe on the following day to do some window-shopping and, for another, she was not particularly fond of Scrabble – she always lost.

"Cheer up, Mum," said Henry. "Come and sit down. Dad's just landed on Northumberland Avenue."

"That's mine," said Emily, managing a smile. "Twelve pounds, please, Albert." She crossed over to the table. But her smile quickly faded as a sudden tattoo of raindrops, fiercer than any that had gone before, hammered on the caravan's fibreglass roof. "I'll tell you who I feel really sorry for, shall I?" she continued, as lightning flashed above the horizon beyond the cliffs. "I pity any poor sailors who are at sea in all of this."

"Seven!" said Albert, as Emily threw a four and a three with the dice. "You've landed on 'Chance'."

Emily picked up a "Chance" card and read out the wording carefully: "*'Go to Jail. Move directly to Jail. Do not pass "Go". Do not collect £200.'*"

"Hard cheese, Mum," said Henry.

"Oh, I don't mind," said Emily, with a little shrug. "It's as good a place to be as any on a night like this."

Hamish McWhister, soaked through to his body despite his oilskins, struggled along the deck of *La Bernache*, his hands and face lashed by the wind and rain. He had to struggle with all his strength to remain upright as the ship pitched and tossed and the sea broke over the side, whipping along the deck and threatening to tug his feet away from under him. Occasionally he would glance over his shoulder and up towards the wheelhouse, fearful that his captain, André Amiens, might catch sight of him.

But the black and starless sky provided excellent cover for the ship's mate. And the captain's constant battle with the storm kept him fully occupied and prevented him from glancing down at the forward deck where McWhister inched his way towards the plastic sheeting that hid the coffin.

Hamish McWhister touched his oilskins, reassuring himself that the axe which he had taken from the fire-point amidships was still securely tucked inside his belt. McWhister's mind was made up. He was going to rid the ship of the coffin and its loathsome contents which had brought nothing but bad luck and were, he was sure, responsible for the awful weather which had dogged *La Bernache*'s progress ever since they had put out from their Continental port.

McWhister rubbed his hands together furiously, in an attempt to bring life back to his frozen fingers. A huge wave broke over the ship's prow, drenching him from head to foot. He grabbed at the plastic sheeting in fear of being carried overboard. Then, as the seawater retreated across the deck, the ship's mate pulled out the red-handled axe and rained down blows on the thick ship's rope which held down the sheeting.

"In heaven's name, man, what are you doing?" Captain Amiens called down at McWhister from the wheelhouse, the words rising and falling on the wind. Amiens' attention had been drawn by the flash of steel as the axe-head swung in the mate's hands. "Stop! Stop! Or I'll have you put in irons!"

But the Scotsman paid not the slightest attention. What he had begun, he intended to finish. Nothing could stop him now. Besides, he knew full well that Amiens had enough on his hands in attempting to keep *La Bernache* from being swamped, and could not leave the ship's wheel. Undeterred by shouted threats, McWhister applied himself all the harder to his task.

Thwock! The first of the two retaining ropes parted at last.

With one rope severed, the second strained with the tautness of a bowstring. It required only a

7

couple of blows to cut it.

Hamish McWhister rocked back on his heels with surprise as the plastic sheeting blew up suddenly in front of his nose and flapped noisily in the high wind like some ghostly black flag. The smooth, shiny black coffin, hidden till now beneath the sheeting, appeared. The ship gave a heaving lurch in the churning sea and the coffin slowly slid across the deck.

At that moment, and for the very first time that night, the moon chose to show itself from behind the scudding storm clouds. As the coffin slid away from him, McWhister had just enough time to make out the lettering on the brass plate which was secured to the coffin lid:

COUNT ALUCARD
The Last Vampire

The coffin picked up speed across the slippery deck and, without pausing, shot over the ship's side into the foam-flecked waters.

"Good riddance to bad rubbish," McWhister muttered and hurled the axe after the coffin. He'd have to face the wrath of his captain but he had no regrets at what he had done. None whatsoever. In fact, he felt very pleased.

It could have been pure coincidence, but at the same moment that the coffin slid over the side and was lost from sight, the wind dropped and the rain slackened off.

Within the hour, the Belgian cargo boat, *La Bernache*, was ploughing a smooth and steady course through a calm and moonlit sea.

"Window-shopping here I come!" murmured Emily Hollins happily, as she laid five rashers of streaky bacon (two each for Albert and Henry and one for herself) in the hot fat sizzling in the frying pan on a gas ring in the tiny, but spotless, kitchen of their caravan holiday home. Inside the oven, four chubby, nicely browned pork sausages (two for Albert and one each for Henry and herself) were nestling side by side, keeping nicely warm on three nicely warmed breakfast plates.

The reason for Emily's happiness was plain. The early morning sun was shining brightly through the kitchen window, and across the de-luxe kitchen fitments. It was shining brightly on the caravan's open-plan lounge which was furnished, as the travel agent's brochure had described it, with luxurious upholstery. It was shining across the caravan's dining area where the table was neatly laid for breakfast.

The sun was streaming, too, across the concreted concourse which surrounded the leisure park's swimming pool on which a discarded salt-and-vinegar crisp packet bobbed merrily.

The sun was also shining on the red-brick restaurant/take-away which was not yet open for business but where, outside the front door, a stray cat was nosing into a greasy paper bag containing a half-eaten cheeseburger and several chips.

The sun was shining, too, on the nine-hole golf course where an early morning middle-aged and portly jogger, Mr Penworthy, resplendent in royal purple jogging suit, red baseball cap and brand new snow-white sneakers, patiently marked time while Sandy, his wheezing cocker spaniel, paused to cock a leg against the metal flag pole which stuck up, at an angle, out of the hole on the first green.

"Come on, boy!" called Mr Penworthy as his dog sneezed, shook himself violently, then scratched at an awkward spot behind his left ear. "Come on, Sandy!" cried Mr Penworthy again and, with an encouraging slap on his thigh, he set off, skirting the golf course, towards the cliff path which led down to the beach and the sea.

Mr Penworthy was both manager and chef at the Scarcombe Caravan Leisure Park's restaurant/take-away. He was also the restaurant/take-away's best customer. Mr Penworthy's addiction to his own burgers was the reason why he was overweight. It was in order to counteract his weight problem that Stanley Penworthy had taken up jogging. Sandy was not half as keen on these early morning exercises as his owner.

"Sandy! *Walkies*, Sandy!" shouted Mr Penworthy over his shoulder.

Sandy sniffed at an old golf ball which was nestling in a bed of dandelions close by the second tee, and pretended not to hear his master's voice. But Sandy knew that the only path to the comfort of his kennel and the delights of his breakfast bowl lay in following his master. So he set off, in his own good time, at a half-hearted lope in pursuit of the purple-suited figure before him.

Back at the Scarcombe Leisure Park, the three

Hollinses were sitting down to breakfast round the table in their caravan's dining area which was, according to the travel agent's brochure, "decorated to the most exacting standards".

"I don't know whether you two bright sparks have got other ideas up your sleeves," said Emily, as Albert and Henry tucked into their fried breakfast, "but do you fancy popping into Scarcombe this morning? We could walk along the front – and then we could do a bit of window-shopping before we contemplate lunch."

"Suits me," said Albert. "I wouldn't say 'no' to a stroll along the prom-prom-prom." He lopped off the end of one of his pork sausages and dipped it into the runny yolk of his fried egg then into the pool of tomato ketchup on the side of his plate. Albert held up the yellowy-browny-reddy titbit on the end of his fork, and studied it admiringly for a second or two: "What do you say, Henry?"

"Sounds great to me," said Henry Hollins. "And then, while you two are looking round the shops, I'll go off and explore the beach."

Albert and Emily Hollins did not reply to this suggestion, but they both raised their eyebrows as they exchanged a glance. Whenever they had been away on holiday and Henry had "gone off exploring", it had usually ended up with them being launched into some unlikely adventure or another.

On one occasion, for instance, Henry Hollins had found a fossilised dinosaur's egg which had later hatched in an airing cupboard. On another visit to the seaside, he had somehow contrived to get himself carried off, over land and sea, in a makeshift balloon fashioned from a wooden hut which was held aloft by gas-filled inflatable toys. There had been one never-to-be-forgotten Hollins family holiday when Henry had managed to get both Emily and Albert transported back in time to King Arthur's Court. And Albert Hollins still got goose pimples whenever he was reminded of the holiday weekend spent in London, when an encounter with a Doctor Jekyll had turned him into a horrible hairy monster . . . But if you are not familiar with these adventures, then you must learn about them in the other Henry Hollins books, for there is neither the time nor space to refer to them at length here.

Henry Hollins's own favourite adventure had taken place during a motoring holiday in Europe when he had visited an ancient, out-of-the way castle, where he had befriended its lonely owner, a vegetarian vampire, the last remaining member of the Dracula family. Being on holiday once again had reminded Henry of that particular encounter, and he wondered what had become of his kindly, misunderstood, gentle-mannered friend. Henry had long since given up any hopes that he might one day meet the fruit-eating Count Alucard again.

"I wonder what he's doing these days?" mused Henry to himself as he munched his breakfast. "I wonder where he is? One thing's certain though, I'll bet he's a million, zillion miles away from here."

Which just goes to prove that you should never take anything for granted.

"Come away from that, Sandy!" called Stanley Penworthy nervously, as his cocker spaniel sniffed at the long black polished rectangular box which had been washed up on to the beach by the morning tide. It was still quite early, and that part of the beach which lay secluded beneath the cliffs was empty apart from the restaurant manager and his inquisitive dog. "*Sandy*! Bad dog, *bad* dog! Heel, boy, *heel*!" cried Mr Penworthy.

But Sandy was a strong contender for the title of "least obedient dog in the world" whenever there was an interesting article to sniff at and investigate. Ignoring his master's calls entirely, Sandy continued to smell his way round the coffin, sniffing with delight the strong scent of the polished wood mixed with various sea smells picked up during its night-time hours afloat. It was a mixture of odours which would have delighted any dog, and Sandy was not the kind of canine to turn his nose up at a good pong.

"Sandy?" Mr Penworthy approached the dog and the long black box with some trepidation.

What on earth could it be? It *looked* like a coffin, yes, but what, after all, would a genuine coffin be doing on Scarcombe sands at this hour of the morning? Or any other hour of the night or day, come to that? No, it was probably part of some practical joke or, perhaps, it had been used in some kind of advertising stunt. Or was it a

14

theatrical prop inadvertently left behind by the makers of some horror film? There must be half a dozen reasonable reasons why he should come across such an object on the beach. But it was certainly *not* a genuine *bona fide* coffin intended for a real live dead person, so he walked close up to the long, black box with scarcely any misgivings, and took hold of Sandy's collar.

"You are a bad, *bad* dog!" scolded Mr Penworthy, waving a reproving forefinger at him. "And if you think you're going to get any Doggy-Treets when we get home, my lad, you've got another—"

But Stanley Penworthy did not finish what he had started to say. For at that moment he was interrupted by a strange, complaining, creaking sound as the coffin's lid, swollen by the long hours it had spent in seawater, groaned slowly upwards. A pale thin hand with long, bony fingers slid delicately along the edge of the coffin and gripped it tightly, the knuckles showing white. Then, as the lid swung fully open to reveal its silver hinges, the coffin's occupant pulled himself up to a sitting position and stared the purple-suited burger-chef full in the face.

Count Alucard, the last in the line of vampires, was as thin and pale as the hand he had used to push open the coffin lid. His lack of colouring contrasted strongly with the black mane of hair which was swept back smoothly from his high forehead. His dark, enquiring eyes were red-rimmed.

"I'm sorry to have to trouble you—" began the Count, politely.

Count Alucard managed no more than seven words when Stanley Penworthy turned on his heel and ran across the empty beach towards the distant promenade. Sandy, sensing that all was not as it should be, scampered along at his master's side for once.

Had Penworthy stayed long enough, he would have seen that the pale-faced gentleman inside the coffin was wearing a black suit and a starched white shirt with a black bow tie. He had a gold medallion on a chain round his neck and, over his shoulders, a scarlet-lined black cloak.

"Oh, dear me!" sighed Count Alucard watching sadly as the purple-suited figure disappeared into the distance. "I seem to have upset someone again."

2

"Pooh!" said Emily Hollins to Henry, tilting her nose disdainfully, and adding: "I don't fancy having haddock and chips in there."

They were looking in the window of the Mermaid Fish and Chip Café, where the cardboard hands on a grease-stained cardboard clock indicated that the café would be open for business at 12.30 p.m., while a lonely bluebottle, trapped between the grimy windowpane and the grubby net curtains, buzzed dolefully and continuously as it tried to escape.

Albert Hollins joined his wife and son, having just left the family car on the cracked concrete of the much graffitied public car park across the road.

"How's about it then?" asked Albert, rubbing his hands together in anticipation of the morning ahead. "Shall we see what Scarcombe has got to offer?"

Not very much, as things turned out. For although the seaside summer season was well under way, the tiny holiday resort was sadly lacking in both visitors and entertainments, as the three Hollinses were quickly to discover as they walked along the seafront.

There was the open-fronted Fun-Time Bingo Parlour, where a sad-faced man, wearing a striped waistcoat and a battered straw hat, sat behind his counter and tried to drum up customers by calling out Bingo numbers into his microphone to a row of empty plastic seats.

Next to the Bingo Parlour stood the bead-curtained booth belonging to the town's fortune-teller, Gypsy Rosa. The booth was surrounded by fading photographs of the Romany lady reading the palms of show-business celebrities of years gone by. The dark-eyed Gypsy Rosa, wearing a shapeless dress, a headscarf and a necklace decorated with gold coins, was leaning against the side of her booth, reading a tattered magazine and drinking ginger beer from a can. She did not glance up as Emily, Albert and Henry strolled past.

A little further along the seafront, past the ornamental gardens where the town's crest, a shrimp and an anchor, was picked out in flowers in a circular flower bed, was the Scarcombe Popular Amusement Park. The Hollinses paused to peer in through the paint-chipped plywood entrance at the park's attractions.

There was a slot-machine arcade where a solitary customer, a woman with a toddler encased in a see-through plastic-covered pushchair, was feeding coins into a glass-fronted machine containing a crane which stubbornly refused to pick up any of the tiny, cheap teddy bears. There was a large roundabout which stood idle for lack of customers but had fairground music blaring out of its loud-speakers. There were several canvas-roofed circular side stalls where the prizes on offer ranged from goldfish in plastic bags to row upon row of hand-painted cocoa-coloured plaster owls and lop-sided black plaster cats.

The only attraction in the park which caught Henry's eye was the Ghost Train, which had a ghastly green-painted frontage decorated with grinning skeletons, witches on broomsticks and Egyptian mummies wrapped in rotting bandages.

"Fancy a gander at the Amusement Park?" asked Albert.

But Henry, having noted that there was a CLOSED card inside the Ghost Train's pay booth, shook his head and made a mental note to come back later, when the only ride that appealed to him was open for business.

There was little on offer for the holiday-maker in Scarcombe, beyond the Amusement Park, except an ice-cream stall, with a white-overalled fat lady in attendance, and a couple of shops, side by side and with identical items in their windows: coloured postcards of the town (mostly showing the ornamental flower gardens); souvenir key-rings; mugs with "A Present From Scarcombe" printed on their sides, and plastic jewellery boxes bedecked with tiny shells.

"It's not really got a great deal going for it, has it, Scarcombe?" said Emily Hollins, despondently, after having spent several minutes staring into the shop windows.

"No," agreed Albert. "There isn't overmuch to write home about, is there?"

"In fact," said Emily, "we've seen just about all that there is to see on the seafront. What do you say to walking up into the town centre, finding somewhere where we can have a sit-down and a cup of coffee and perhaps a packet of ginger biscuits to share between us?"

"That might just pass half an hour or so," said Albert, hopefully, but he was already beginning to wonder how on earth they were going to pass the next two weeks of their holiday. "Would that suit you, Henry?"

21

But Henry's attention had been drawn to a knot of about twenty holiday-makers standing in a circle round something on the sand. Henry wondered what Scarcombe beach had got to offer that could attract so many people. He decided to investigate, and arranged to meet his parents at twelve o'clock, sharp, outside the Fish and Chip Café – the one with the captive bluebottle in the window. Henry scampered across the beach towards the ring of holiday-makers.

"Move along! Do move along there!" snapped Police Constable Norman Woolley, sitting on the empty coffin, waving his hands at the circle of holiday-makers which surrounded him. "Come on!" he pleaded. "Smartly does it! Move along! There's nothing here worth looking at!"

Constable Woolley was wrong, of course. There was something very much worth looking at. Himself. For it is not every day that you see a policeman sitting on a coffin on the beach.

The constable thought very hard, wondering what to do next. The onlookers showed no signs of dispersing. Things might have been different if he could have stood up. The reason that the holiday-makers weren't taking him seriously, he decided, was because he was sitting down, particularly as he happened to be sitting on a coffin. Police Constable Woolley looked downright silly, and he knew it. But if he stood up now, the holiday-makers would be able to read the brass plate on the coffin lid, and that was the very last thing the constable wanted to happen.

"Get yourself down there pronto, Woolley!" Police Sergeant Downend had told him, when it had first been reported at the station that there was a vampire's coffin on the beach. "And whatever you do, don't let it get about that it's supposed to belong to Dracula."

"Dracula, Sarge?" Constable Woolley had murmured with a shudder. "The chap that goes round biting people's necks? Yerks! It doesn't really belong to him, does it?"

"No, you crackpot!" the sergeant had thundered. "Of course it doesn't! There are no such things as vampires. Everybody knows that. It's probably just a silly prank. It's probably those polytechnic students up to their tricks again. But if the rumour was to spread round the town that there was a vampire on the loose, it wouldn't do much for the holiday trade, would it?"

"No, Sarge."

"The mayor would go bananas. The town council would go completely off their chumps. And who'd get the blame for it, do you think?"

"Dunno, Sarge."

"Why, we would, of course, you duffer. So just keep that bit of information about Dracula strictly under wraps. Got it?"

"Got it, Sarge."

But when the police constable had arrived on the otherwise still empty beach, it was to discover the brass plate on the coffin lid staring him in the face.

"Oh, crumbs!" muttered Woolley to himself. "If anybody spots that, I'm done for. The sarge will have my boots for loaf-tins."

He had glanced towards the promenade and seen the first of the morning's holiday-makers venturing down the wooden steps and on to the beach. He would have to do something quickly before the cat got out of the bag. Police Constable Woolley had acted upon a sudden decision. He had done the only thing possible to keep the brass plate from the public's gaze. He had sat on it.

Almost an hour later, he was still sitting on the coffin, surrounded by inquisitive holiday-makers, when Henry Hollins arrived at the back of the crowd. He wriggled past a lady carrying a child's inflatable rubber ring shaped like a duck, and a tall man wearing a red bow tie with white spots and holding up a large, important-looking camera, and made his way to the front.

"Stop that!" cried Constable Woolley, as the man with the spotted bow tie took his photograph. The constable instantly recognised Nigel Protheroe, chief photographer on the Scarcombe Evening Chronicle. He had taken Woolley's photograph once before when he had been appearing as a member of the Scarcombe Formation Dancing Team. They had very nearly won through the heat that would have taken them on

24

to fame, fortune and an appearance on television's *Come Dancing* programme. Formation dancing was Constable Woolley's hobby.

"Give us a big smile, Constable," said Protheroe, ignoring the policeman's order and preparing to take a second photograph.

Police Constable Woolley covered his face with his helmet and hoped against hope that Nigel would go away and leave him alone. "I wish I was somewhere else," the constable muttered into his helmet. "I wish I was miles away from here."

But if Dame Fate was not going to whisk the policeman away to a happier place, she was not going to let him down entirely. Help was at hand.

"All right, that'll do! Shove off, the lot of you!" It was the authoritative voice of Police Sergeant Downend. "That goes for you as well, Mr Protheroe," the sergeant went on sternly, as the camera clicked away, this time to record the arrival of the police sergeant and the four constables accompanying him. They had come to carry the coffin off and away from prying eyes.

As the circle of holiday-makers broke up, Henry Hollins moved with them. But he did not go very far. There was something about the coffin that stirred a chord in his memory.

Henry squatted down close to the water's edge, some twenty metres away from the coffin and the group of policemen, and pretended to study a jellyfish washed up on the beach.

"All right, Woolley, lad," said the sergeant, with a jerk of his thumb at the coffin. "Up on your feet, and give these lads a hand to haul it back across the beach. We've got a van parked up on the promenade to take it back to the station."

"I can't get up, Sarge," hissed Woolley, nodding across at the photographer who was pretending to take a photograph of two children who were building a sandcastle. "There's a brass plate on the coffin lid," the constable continued. "It says 'Count Alucard' on it. If that nosy parker should chance to see it, we'd really be in trouble."

"Count Alucard? Who's he?" asked Sergeant Downend.

"It's Dracula, Sarge, spelled backwards," whispered the constable.

"Good heavens, Woolley, so it is!" gasped Downend. "You stay exactly where you are with your bottom parked on that brass plate. These other chaps can carry you *and* the coffin." The sergeant beckoned to the four waiting policemen and pointed at the coffin. "Altogether, lads – shoulders to it – *heave!*"

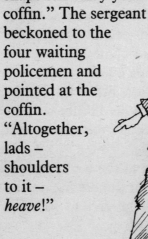

The four policemen positioned themselves, one at each corner of the coffin and, with their fellow-constable perched awkwardly atop, lifted it up on to their shoulders.

"By the right – quick march!" called the sergeant.

Then, with Downend striding smartly out in front, the four constables set off carrying their burden, staggering slightly on the loose sand, towards the wooden steps which led up to the promenade.

Click! and *Click!* again, went the shutter on Nigel Protheroe's camera as he sneaked a couple of shots of the policemen making clumsy progress across the uneven sand with their burden.

Henry Hollins stood up and, leaving the land-locked jellyfish to an uncertain fate, set off slowly towards the esplanade. He was still deep in thought. He was sure he recognised the coffin and he was pretty certain, too, what the constable was concealing by sitting on the lid.

"Pickled gherkin?"

"No, ta very much."

"Onion slice?"

It was 12.15 p.m., and the Caravan Leisure Park's restaurant/take-away was open for business. Stanley Penworthy, now in his white chef's overall and cap, was attending to the needs of his first customer. But Penworthy was not his usual expert self. His hand was shaking as he handed the quarter-pound cheeseburger across the counter to the young man in the belted raincoat.

"Are you all right?" asked the young man in the raincoat.

"Smashing," lied Penworthy. "Why do you ask?"

"You're trembling," said the young man in the raincoat, nodding at the hand which had passed him the cheeseburger.

"Ah," said the chef with an uneasy grin, "thereby hangs a tale."

"Go on."

"Just one tiny moment," said Penworthy, as the door opened and a boy walked in. "Yes, young man, and what can I do for you?"

"Can I have two cheeseburgers, one baconburger and two helpings of chips, please, to take away?"

"Coming up," said Mr Penworthy. Henry paid and was on his way back to the Hollins's caravan with their greasy lunch. Mr Penworthy put the money into the till, whistling tunelessly.

"Go on," said the young man in the raincoat.

Stanley Penworthy shook his head. "I wish I could, but I can't," he said. "My lips are sealed."

"Come again? I don't understand," said the young man, carefully picking a slice of pickled gherkin out of his cheeseburger and dropping it in the waste-bin.

"I am sorry," said Mr Penworthy. "You definitely said 'no gherkin', didn't you?"

"No harm done," said the young man in the raincoat with a friendly grin.

"To be quite honest," said the chef, "I don't know whether I'm coming or going this morning." He rubbed the back of one hand wearily across his forehead, then, feeling a sudden urge to confide in someone, he added: "Can I tell you a secret?"

"Of course."

"Only I promised the police sergeant that I wouldn't breathe a word, but if I don't talk to somebody soon, I'll go mad."

"You can trust me," said the young man.

"It all began," said Mr Penworthy, "when I went for my daily jog this morning on the sands. You'll never guess, not in a million years, what I saw on the beach."

"Go on," said the young man in the raincoat, leaning across the counter and swallowing the last mouthful of cheeseburger. "I'm listening." But as he spoke, and unseen by the chef, the young man slipped his hand into his pocket and switched on the midget tape-recorder he had concealed inside his raincoat.

For the young man was none other than Royston Renshaw, reporter on the *Scarcombe Evening Chronicle*, and a colleague of Nigel Protheroe.

If the restaurant chef was looking for someone whom he could trust to share a secret, he had chosen exactly the wrong man.

VAMPIRE IN SCARCOMBE!

it said in huge, black letters across the top of the front page of that evening's *Chronicle*, and underneath that, in slightly smaller letters,

Authority's Eerie Silence

And underneath that subheading was Nigel's photograph of the four policemen carrying the coffin across the sands, with a fifth policeman perched on top. Underneath the photograph, in still smaller letters, was written:

What is the story behind the sinister coffin, pictured above, which was washed up by the tide on Scarcombe's beach this morning? Where are the four policemen taking it to? Why is there a fifth policeman sitting on top of it? Is it to prevent someone – or something – trapped inside the coffin from getting out? Is there, in fact, an evil, blood-drinking monster lurking within the dreadful box? The police authorities refuse to say. But the Scarcombe Evening Chronicle, *your campaigning newspaper, believes that its readers deserve to know the full facts! Turn to page three and read Royston Renshaw's exclusive interview with the man who came face to face with the vampire – and who has lived to tell the tale!*

"Brrrr! Vampires!" Albert Hollins gave a little shiver, although the late afternoon sun was still blazing down, and glanced nervously around.

There really wasn't anything to be afraid of. Albert was sitting in a deck chair, with Emily beside him, by the side of the leisure park's concrete-terraced swimming pool. The salt-and-vinegar crisp packet, which had floated merrily on the pool at early morning, had been removed by the eagle-eyed pool attendant and the clear, blue waters were thronged with holiday-makers, both young and old, who swam, or floated, or tossed inflated beach balls to each other, or scrambled out and made dripping pilgrimages either to the refreshment kiosk or the toilets – and sometimes both.

Albert Hollins had driven down into the town not long before and bought his *Evening Chronicle* from the newspaperman who stood at the foot of the crumbling Clock Tower opposite the ornamental gardens. It was the first evening paper to arrive in the leisure park and, consequently, the other holiday-makers were entirely unaware of the possible presence of a vampire in Scarcombe.

There was, therefore, a cheerful, carefree, holiday atmosphere round the swimming pool. But reading about the vampire on the front page of his newspaper had caused Albert Hollins to shiver all down his body, from the white handkerchief, knotted at all four corners, on the top of his head, right down to the tips of his green-socked toes which peeped out from his sandals.

"Brrrrr!" Albert shivered again and then glanced, first at Emily who was reading a women's magazine article called *How to Brighten Up Your Plant Pots*, and then across at Henry who was sitting in his swimming trunks, dangling his feet in the pool, thoughtfully sipping at a fizzy drink.

Henry Hollins, like his father, was concerned about the vampire stories. He had been worrying over them ever since coming back from the beach that morning. He had managed to sneak a glance at the front page of his father's evening paper and, taking one thing with another, had realised that there was more than enough cause for concern.

But Henry was not worried on his own account. No, he was only concerned about the vampire's safety. If there *was* any truth in the rumours that were beginning to drift around the town and if there really *was* a vampire at large in Scarcombe, then it would be that vampire's life that would be in danger, and not the lives of the townspeople and holiday-makers.

For it was Henry's belief that the vampire in question could very well be his old friend, Count Alucard, and for Henry Hollins, vampires were an endangered species. Count Alucard himself had once told Henry that he was the very last in the line of Dracula vampires – in which circumstance, how could this vampire be any other? And the Count Alucard that Henry knew, and treasured as a friend, was a vegetarian vampire who, when he was transformed into a bat, had never sunk his fangs into anything more sinister than a juicy orange or a luscious plum.

But in spite of his shy and friendly nature and his vegetarian diet, Count Alucard had been forced to flee from the European castle that was his home, in order to escape the wrath of the local villagers whose ignorance made them go in fear of him.

"And I'll bet that the very same thing will happen to him all over again here," thought Henry gloomily. He took another swig at his fizzy drink and disconsolately dangled his toes in the swimming pool, and then added, fiercely: "But not if I can help it!"

3

"Ah-whoooOOOO!"

The strange animal baying rose and fell on the late afternoon breeze. The two men stopped arguing and exchanged an anxious glance.

"Ah-whoooOOOO!"

Again the howling drifted in through the open window of the police station.

"Listen!" said Cyril Lightowler, none other than the mayor of Scarcombe, a short, chubby, bald-headed snappily dressed man. "There it goes again!"

"It's the wolves, Mr Mayor," said Sergeant Downend. "Up at the zoo. The sound carries down the cliffs. Sometimes, when the wind's in this direction, we can pong them as well." He paused, wrinkled his nose distastefully and continued: "They ought to have closed it down, that zoo, yonks ago—"

"I know they're the wolves!" snapped the town's mayor, flapping a hand at the sergeant and cutting him short. "What I want to know is, what are they howling *for*?"

"Dunno," said Sergeant Downend, with a shrug. "Perhaps they're hungry."

"I'll tell you what they're howling for," snapped the mayor, deciding to answer his own question. "They know that there's a vampire in the town. They have this sort of eerie understanding, vampires and wolves – I saw it in an old movie once, on the telly—"

"*Ah-whoooOOOOOO!*"

"They know that there's a vampire all right," murmured the mayor uneasily, running a forefinger round the inside of his collar, which was sticking to his neck with perspiration. "Where is it, Sergeant? Which cell have you got it locked up in?"

"There is no vampire in this police station," replied Sergeant Downend. "How many times do I have to tell you, Mr Mayor? We have no vampire on these premises and we never have had one!"

"Then how do you explain this, Sergeant?" demanded the mayor, thrusting the front page of the *Scarcombe Evening Chronicle* under the station sergeant's nose and jabbing a finger at the picture. "What's that young copper sitting up there for, if it's not to keep the occupant safely shut up inside? Are you telling me that you had the vampire contained, and you've let it get away?"

As well as being mayor of Scarcombe, Cyril Lightowler was also the owner of both the slot-machine arcade in the Amusement Park and one of the two gift shops on the seafront. He was deeply concerned about what would happen to the tourist trade and, subsequently, the takings at both of his business ventures, when the word got round that the town had its own resident vampire.

"There isn't any vampire!" insisted Sergeant Downend. "And there wasn't anything in the coffin when those policemen carried it off – it was Constable Woolley's own initiative that made him sit on top of it. He didn't want to alarm anyone. There's a brass plate on the coffin lid. It's got 'Count Alucard' engraved on it."

"Count Alucard?"

"Yes," said the sergeant. "It's . . . it's Dracula backwards. We were trying to keep it a secret."

"Good grief, Sergeant!" groaned the mayor. "Then it *is* a vampire's coffin! Trying to keep it a secret, were you? You didn't make a very good job of it then! You've managed to get it splashed across the front page of the local rag! And what about this burger-chef chap up at the Caravan Leisure Park who's given the interview?"

"Him! The less said about him the better," growled the sergeant. "He was the one who came in here and reported it in the first place. I gave him very strict instructions not to mention it to a soul – and then he goes and blabs it out to the newspaper."

"But if he actually *saw* this vampire—"

"He didn't see a vampire. There isn't any vampire. He saw somebody dressed up as a vampire, that's all. If you want my opinion, it was one of them students from the polytechnic, as I was saying to—"

"If I want your opinion, Sergeant, I'll ask for it," snapped the mayor. "And whether it's a real vampire or a pretend one, it needs a stop putting to it. It's gone too far as it is. The tourists will be leaving Scarcombe in droves once they've seen this evening's paper. And what's the council going to say when they get to hear about it? I've a council meeting in the morning – they'll go stark staring round the twist! I want results, Sergeant. I want every man you've got out there looking for this Alucard chap, be he a joker or a genuine vampire – I want him brought in. Understood?"

"I'm not entirely without initiative myself, Mr Mayor," said the station sergeant, crossly. "I've got every available man scouring the town this very minute. Along the beach, underneath the pier, inside the shelters in the ornamental gardens. And they've got very strict orders not to pack up looking until it's dark. Why, I even had to make my own cup of tea this afternoon, because there was nobody here to—"

"Not to pack it in until when, did you say, Sergeant?" the mayor interrupted frostily.

"Until it gets too dark to look," repeated the station sergeant.

The mayor's eyes narrowed and his cheeks reddened as he strove to contain his temper. "Vampires only come out when it's dark, you duffer!" he snarled. "That's the time to *look* for vampires – when it's night-time – not to *stop* looking. You can tell your men to stay out there tonight – all night, if necessary, until that evil monster's safely behind bars. And you'd better stay here in the station and control the search."

"What? Stop up all night?" the station sergeant's eyebrows shot up in alarm. The afternoon was beginning to drift into early evening. Through the open window, Sergeant Downend could see the sun dipping behind the horizon. Already the shadows were lengthening in the police station. The sergeant knew, from previous experience, that there was one particular corner of that room where the glow from the single electric light bulb over the counter did not reach. It was possible to imagine all kinds of weird and scary creatures skulking in that dark corner. Particularly if he was ever in the station on his own. Besides, all this talk of vampires was beginning to set his nerves on edge. Not that he believed in vampires . . . But the idea of spending the entire night in the station all alone did not appeal to him. All the same, he wasn't going to admit it.

"Are you sure that's absolutely necessary, Mr Mayor?" asked the station sergeant. "We still don't know for certain that this vampire exists, and personally speaking, I don't think—"

"*Ah-whoooOOOO!*" Once again the howls from the wolf pack drifted in through the police-station window, sounding a little bit spookier than before.

"You may not think that there's a vampire out there, Sergeant," said the mayor. "But I happen to think that those wolves know better than you."

"*Ah-whoooOOO!*"

Henry Hollins threw back the duvet, scrambled up on to his knees, drew back the curtain and peered out through his bedroom window into the night.

Scarcombe Wildlife Zoo lay just beyond the Caravan Leisure Park and the constant howling of the wolves was preventing Henry from sleeping. It had started to rain again. Not the furious, gale-tossed, driving rain of the previous night, but a steady, heavy, unremitting downpour. There was a full moon, too, peeping through the black clouds and over the tips of the tallest pine trees in the sparsely wooded wolf compound.

Henry sat quite still, listening to the rain drumming on the fibreglass roof and looking across towards the high, wire-mesh fence behind which prowled the restless wolf pack. Count Alucard had not been out of Henry's thoughts all night. He wondered where his vegetarian-vampire friend was, and dearly hoped that if, as he supposed, the Count was somewhere close at hand, he had managed to find some shelter from the rain. Henry would have liked to have gone out, rain or no rain, and searched the night for Count Alucard. But commonsense told him that it would prove an impossible task.

"Ah-whoooOOO!"

"This is daft!" muttered Police Constable Norman Woolley to himself, as he pulled his rain-cape up round his ears and for reassurance felt the handle of his truncheon. Wet, miserable, and more than a little uneasy, Constable Woolley was stumbling through the long grass outside the zoo, hoping against hope that he would not come into contact with the vampire he had been instructed to arrest.

Just his luck to get landed with the zoo beat! His colleague, Constable Les Collins, had been despatched to patrol the area beneath the pier, which would shelter him from the rain. Police Constable Barncastle, another close acquaintance, had been sent to search the ornamental gardens where there was an imitation Chinese pagoda which would also keep the rain off. But Woolley's luck, as usual, had run out, and he had been given the zoo patrol, which stretched for miles and was dark and lonely.

"*Ah-whoooOOO!*"

Another wolf call, and this time only a couple of metres away, made Woolley almost jump out of his skin. The young policeman swallowed nervously, then, praying that the perimeter fence had not got any holes in it, he quickened his pace.

Boris, the scrawny leader of the mangy, flea-ridden pack of wolves that roamed the compound, licked at a scar – a relic from a long-forgotten fight – just above his right front paw and then, shaking the rain from his patchy fur, flung back his scruffy head and howled loud and long for the umpteenth time that night.

"*Ah-whoooOOOO!*"

A trio of younger wolves, Igor, Ivan and Kevin,

skulking in a nearby thicket, peered warily across at Boris and then, simultaneously, all three echoed the cry:

"Ah-whoooOOOOO!"

At that, three young she-wolves, Olga, Dushka and Tracey, lying half-asleep on a patch of grass they were intending to keep dry, blinked, yawned and promptly closed their eyes again.

Boris, however, was fully awake. Galvanised by a curious energy he did not comprehend, he set off, tongue lolling and panting quickly, padding at speed across a thin carpet of pine needles close to the perimeter fence.

The old wolf was one of the few surviving pack members from the many that had been trapped in the forests of Central Europe years before, and shipped across the English Channel when the Scarcombe Wildlife Zoo had been put together. Most of the other wolves in the present pack had been born inside the compound.

But out of all of the pack, Boris was the only wolf who remembered the meaning of freedom.

Old though he was, he could still remember the unending forests, the vast, snow-covered wastes and the tall mountain ranges of his native land. He could recall, with wonder, what it was like to run as far and for as long as he desired – without coming up against a wire-mesh fence. He could remember, too, the keen joy of the chase and the fierce pleasure of the kill. In those far-off, never-to-be-forgotten days, he had run with a wolf pack that had had pride and comradeship – a pack

41

where every wolf ran hard and not only for itself but for its fellows.

Boris would have liked to have been able to explain all this to the other members of the pack. But how can you explain the taste of meat you have freshly killed yourself, to a wolf brought up on frozen joints tossed over the fence by man? How do you explain the meaning of freedom to a wolf born and raised in captivity?

At the end of the perimeter fence, Boris turned and, without pausing, set off back the way he had come, loping along at speed and with regular bounding strides, his haunches brushing the wire mesh. There was a deep and indefinable yearning in the pit of his stomach, a hunger for the old days that he had not felt for years. The old pack leader did not know the cause of this longing. It was at one and the same time both pleasurable and hurtful.

Neither did he know that, high in the treetops above his head, a furry-bodied, sharp-toothed, blunt-nosed creature of the night was soaring and swooping on long, slender, dark, parchment-like wings. It was a fruit-eating vampire bat and it was, in some way, responsible for the old wolf's yearnings.

The mayor of Scarcombe, Cyril Lightowler, had told nothing less than the truth when he said to the police-station sergeant that there was an eerie understanding between vampires and wolves.

Count Alucard, for it was none other than he that dived and banked and darted in his bat form above the wolves' compound, also felt a strange compulsion. The wolf pack in the zoo reminded him of his European homeland. It reminded him of his castle, now destroyed, and the wooded mountain slopes where, as a child, he had laughed and played and run and, later, grown to manhood. The Count was tempted to stay, swooping and diving, darting and gliding, on outstretched bat-wings in and around the treetops.

But commonsense urged him to move on. He would need to find a place where he could shelter for the night and where, when morning came, he could safely return to human form. Count Alucard flapped his slender wings and headed off, skimming across and away from the zoo, over the cliff tops and towards the town.

"This isn't half bad!" yawned Police Constable Barncastle to himself, as he leaned back on the red and gold oriental seat and listened to the rain pitter-pattering overhead on the several roofs of the imitation Chinese pagoda. The constable flicked on his torch and shone it on to his watch. It was exactly three a.m. With any luck, the rain would stop long before the sun came up. Another three hours to kill in the shelter of the pagoda, then it would be time to stroll back to the police station, sign his name in the duty book, and go off home to the appetising breakfast of crispy bacon and runny fried egg that his mother always cooked for him.

"Yes," murmured the policeman, "life could be a whole lot worse!" He closed his eyes, wrinkled his forehead and then continued to himself: "I spy with my little eye, something beginning with C."

It was his own version of "I-Spy" which he often played by himself to while away the lonely night-beat hours. It was a kind of "I-Spy" in reverse. He thought of a letter of the alphabet first, and then looked round for an object beginning with that letter.

Constable Barncastle opened his eyes and looked round the pagoda. He smiled to himself. It was too easy. There were lots of things on every side of him that began with C. "Chinese pagoda." "Chinese seat." "Chinese scroll." "Chinese screen." "Chinese pagoda floor." It was cheating in a way, he told himself. Still, if he was only cheating himself, there wasn't really any harm in

44

it. He switched his torch on again and shone it upwards.

"'Chinese pagoda ceiling'," added the policeman, before his jaw dropped open and his eyes bulged with fear. "Crikey Moses!" he gasped.

High in the rafters above his head fluttered a grim night-time creature, with long, dark, membranous wings, black beady eyes and pointed teeth which glinted in the beam of light from his torch.

"Yeeeaaagh!" Constable Barry Barncastle let out a fearful scream as he leapt to his feet and tore out of the pagoda.

He sped the length of the ornamental gardens in record time – he had not been chosen to represent his station in the two hundred metres sprint at the forthcoming Policemen's Regional Sports Day for nothing! – and slumped against the concrete gateposts, gulping as he regained his breath and trying, desperately, to collect his thoughts.

Had he *really* seen a vampire bat fluttering in the rafters? Might it not have been a trick of the light? Or could it, possibly, have been one of the many Chinese carvings that he had caught in the beam of his torch? Was it not his duty as an officer of the law to go back and investigate further? Of course it was! And that was exactly what he would do.

At that point Constable Barncastle realised that, in his headlong flight, he had dropped his torch on the floor of the pagoda.

"Oh, well, that does it, Barry," he told himself. "I'm certainly not venturing into that pagoda in the dark to look for it! I shall just have to wait and see if anyone hands it in at the Lost Property Office."

But what was he going to tell his station sergeant now? He could hardly admit that, instead of following orders and searching the ornamental gardens, he had sheltered from the rain inside the Chinese pagoda. Neither could he admit that he had passed the time by playing "I-Spy With My Little Eye" by himself. No, it would have to be a case of least said soonest mended.

That decided, he set off again along the promenade in search of alternative shelter for the remaining hours of darkness. Shrugging off the memory of his recent nasty encounter, Barncastle smiled to himself as he remembered the doorway of the two seafront gift shops – just the place to pass a pleasant hour or so.

The policeman knew from past experience that the moonlit shop windows were nothing less than treasure-houses for the solo player at "I-Spy With My Little Eye". He would begin with the letter S, he promised himself. There was a rich seam to be mined of items beginning with S: "souvenir key-rings", "seashell-covered jewellery boxes", "seaside postcards", "Scarcombe souvenir mugs" . . .

There was a jaunty spring in Barry Barncastle's step as he strode out along the promenade. He was whistling a merry tune to himself under his breath.

Back in the Chinese pagoda, Count Alucard, still in his bat form, took a firm but delicate grip with his needle-sharp claws on one of the highest rafters. He lowered himself gently into his upside-down position, enveloped his furry body with his batwings, closed his black, beady eyes, and promptly fell asleep.

4

"The Dobsons are leaving," said Henry Hollins glumly as he watched a small green family car, loaded down with passengers and luggage, move out of the leisure park.

The Dobsons were a jolly family: mother, father, four children and a large, lolloping and incredibly clumsy dog. Henry had made friends with the dog called Arthur by the swimming pool on the previous afternoon. It had knocked over his fizzy drink, put several muddy paw marks on

his clean towel and licked his face all over with lots of enthusiasm and a rough tongue. Henry's encounter with Arthur had led to his making friends with Richard, Emma, Amy and Ben. Henry, who did not usually make friends all that easily, had been overjoyed at finding five new ones in one afternoon.

Alas though, it now seemed as if it had been a case of easy come, easy go. The Dobson family were leaving the leisure park seven days earlier than they had originally intended.

"Oh dear me," said Emily Hollins, with a sigh. "Are they hopping it as well?"

"So it would seem," replied Albert. "That's the third family that's left in the last half hour."

For the second day in succession, the previous night's rain had eased before dawn which had brought with it the sun. It had been a bright enough sun to lure the Hollins family out of doors to eat their breakfast under the striped awning of their caravan. But it was not proving to be as pleasant an experience as they had hoped. They had sat and watched as several of their fellow holiday-makers had packed their things, loaded their car boots and roof racks, and driven out of the camp. A lot of people, it seemed, were worried about the possible presence of a vampire in Scarcombe.

The story had been picked up by both television and the national press – not that either had taken it too seriously. The presenter on the TV breakfast programme had held up the copy of the *Scarcombe*

Evening Chronicle, showing the notorious picture, and read out the details with a twinkle in his eye. The national newspapers had also treated the vampire story as something of a joke.

But if the national press and the TV people were prepared to regard the possibility of a vampire with a pinch of salt, the residents and the holiday-makers in Scarcombe were concerned for their livelihoods or their lives.

"There's one good thing to be said for all these people slinging their hooks this morning," said Albert Hollins, hoping to cheer up his wife and son. "I'll bet there won't be a queue to get on the first tee of that nine-hole golf course. Who fancies a round of golf?"

"Count me out, Albert," said Emily. "I've got to write my postcards this morning."

"But we only got here yesterday," replied Albert, looking puzzled. "Can't the postcards wait for a day or two?"

Emily shook her head. "I always like to get them off in good time, Albert, you know that. Otherwise, you find yourself getting home before the postcards have been delivered. And then it's a question of folk saying: 'My, you do look brown! Have you been on your holidays?' – 'Yes, we've been to Scarcombe. Didn't you get our card?' – 'No? Why? Did you send us one?' – 'Yes. A shiny coloured picture of the ornamental gardens in full bloom.' – 'Well, it certainly hasn't come.' No, Albert, I'd rather get the postcards off today, and save possible embarrassment."

50

"Suit yourself," replied Albert, with a little shrug. "How about you, Henry? Do you want a game of golf?"

"No, thanks, Dad," said Henry. "I'd rather go down into the town again this morning, if it's all the same to you. There's something I want to do."

"Just as you wish," replied Albert, cheerfully. "I shall go round the course on my own – it'll give me the chance to get some practice in before I wallop the pair of you."

Henry was delighted at having the matter settled without argument. He wanted the morning to himself. Having lain awake and listened help-lessly to the howling of the wolves the night before, he was more determined than ever to find his friend, Count Alucard.

"The only problem now," mused Henry Hol-lins, "is where do I begin to look?"

Count Alucard adjusted his black bow tie and then smoothed back his dark, shiny, hair behind his ears with the palms of his hands. He lifted the gold medallion on the chain round his neck, breathed on it hard and then polished it with his handkerchief until it shone and sparkled in the morning sunlight. Only then, when he was satis-fied that he was as smart as could be expected, did he peer, warily, round the carved and gilded wooden wall of the Chinese pagoda.

A squirrel scampered over a dew-wet, neatly trimmed lawn, pausing halfway across to sit up on its haunches, cast darting glances all round, and then continue on its way towards the shelter of some beeches. A goldfinch twittered on the branch of a nearby hazel tree. A bumblebee buzzed lazily round a well-kept flower bed. Over on the lily pond, a frog sat on a broad leaf and swivelled its eyes in search of breakfast.

There was as yet no sign of human life in the ornamental gardens. But the Count knew that this good luck could not last, and that before long the gardens would be invaded by the morning's rash of tourists and day trippers. And, worse still, the police would soon return to track him down.

Count Alucard knew that he was a wanted man. After his unfortunate encounter with the man and the dog on the beach the previous morning, the vegetarian vampire Count had taken to his heels and hidden away, all through the previous day, in a clump of bushes high up on the cliffs. The same friendly bushes that sheltered him had also provided him with a meal of berries. A discarded newspaper had blown his way during the early evening and, to his horror and amazement, he had discovered that he was front page news.

Count Alucard let out a long, sad sigh and pondered on his predicament. It had not been a good idea, he now decided, to have himself shipped over to England in his comfortable coffin for a few weeks' holiday. He had intended to go to Whitby, where his great-grandfather had once gone before him, but had been cast up instead on the unfamiliar beach of a seedy, run-down seaside town.

But there was no way now of going back – or of going on to Whitby. He wouldn't dream of going anywhere without his precious coffin. And now he didn't even know where his coffin was.

He had watched, in open-mouthed astonishment, as the policemen had carried it across the beach. They had no right to deprive him of it! It was his personal, private property. It was not theirs to touch. It had been carved for him, with love and care, by an old Transylvanian carpenter. It had been padded and lined with snow-white satin by the undertaker in his native village. It was *his* coffin. It *belonged* to him. It had been taken away and he had no idea how to get it back.

But that would have to wait. First things first. He needed to find a safe haven. The clump of bushes had served its purpose. But now he needed somewhere more comfortable and more permanent. And he needed to act quickly . . .

The Count's eyes roamed round the area beyond the ornamental gardens to the seashore and the promenade. But these were both coming to life, and he could hear the sounds of cars along the promenade road, the cries of the fishermen and the calling of the seagulls from the tiny harbour. He dared not venture out, dressed as he was, for fear of being instantly recognised.

Glancing next to the left side of the gardens, he made out the maze of narrow shopping streets beyond the privet hedge. He then looked over towards the right hand side of the gardens to the town's amusement park. He could see the Big

Wheel, motionless now, rising high over the canvas roofs of the stalls and sideshows. He could also make out the Giant Merry-Go-Round, its gaily painted horses still, and the ancient fairground organ silent.

The Scarcombe Amusement Park had not opened for business.

Count Alucard took a last look all around the ornamental gardens and then, having made up his mind about which direction he would take, strode out through the arched opening of the Chinese pagoda, leapt nimbly over the KEEP OFF THE GRASS sign and sped over the neatly trimmed lawns and well-kept flower beds, the scarlet lining of his cloak spreading out behind him as he ran.

"Haven't you any idea at all where he might be hiding?" asked Cyril Lightowler, mopping his brow with a big red-and-white-spotted handkerchief.

It was not just the uncomfortable heat from the electric fire in the cramped, bead-curtained confines of the gypsy fortune-teller's booth that had made the beads of sweat ooze out of his forehead and drip down the mayoral nose. No, Cyril Lightowler was perspiring mostly because he was deeply worried about the effect of the vampire rumours on the town.

"There's nothing there!" announced the fortune-teller firmly, and the gold coins rattled on her necklace as she gazed at the mayor over the

top of her crystal ball. "The crystal refuses to reveal to us where the vampire is hiding."

"Are you *sure?*" asked the mayor, gnawing anxiously at his lower lip. "Give it another go."

But as the gypsy's scarf-covered head bent over her crystal ball for a second attempt at locating the vampire, Cyril Lightowler knew, in his heart of hearts, that there was little chance of any success. He hadn't really expected that Gypsy Rosa would be able to help him, but he did not know where else to turn. He had just come round from the police station which he had found locked, with a note pinned to the door:

> Two pints of green-top and a
> carton of raspberry yoghourt,
> please, Mr Milkman.

Having been on duty all night, Police Sergeant Downend had stood down his police force and gone home for a few hours' well-earned sleep.

"That's great!" Cyril Lightowler grumbled as he stared at the scrap of paper. "The town is being terrorised by a vampire, and all Sergeant Downend cares about is ordering the milk for his cocoa!"

So, very nearly at his wits' end, and like a drowning man clutching at a straw, the mayor of Scarcombe sought out the help of Gypsy Rosa.

Before he left home that morning, his telephone had rung constantly with calls from hoteliers and guesthouse-keepers – and there had been one too from the manager of the Caravan Leisure Park – all of them complaining that their visitors were packing up, settling their accounts, and leaving Scarcombe because of the rumour. He also knew that he would have some awkward questions to answer at the town council meeting later that day, for most of his fellow councillors, like himself, had businesses which were dependent on the tourist trade.

But, worst of all by far, if the vampire wasn't found and apprehended, the mayor knew that he would have to face the wrath of his wife again.

"It's absolutely ridiculous, Cyril, having a vampire in Scarcombe, and particularly in the middle of the holiday season," Mrs Lightowler had snapped at breakfast, spooning marmalade thickly on to her toast. "They wouldn't put up with one at Blackpool! There was never a monster in

Mablethorpe! Ventnor wouldn't countenance a vampire! Do you think that they would so much as allow Count Dracula to enter Clacton-on-Sea?"

"They let him into Whitby," the mayor had mumbled over his cornflakes in reply.

"Who?"

"Count Dracula. It's in the book. I got it out of the library. He went to Whitby once."

"When?"

"A long time ago."

"Well, he isn't there now, is he?" the mayoress had replied, angrily. "He's here! We've been lumbered with him. And I want to know what you're going to do about it. I've got an important civic function to attend this afternoon: I'm judging the Glamorous Granny Contest on the pier. But there wasn't so much as a mention of it on the local radio this morning. All they could find to talk about was your wretched vampire!"

"It isn't *my* vampire, Dora—"

"It doesn't matter who it belongs to, Cyril!" the mayoress interrupted. "And I don't know how you can just sit there, chomping cornflakes," she had continued, speaking herself through a mouthful of toast and marmalade. "Get out of the house and *do* something! And see to it that the blood-drinking monster is got rid of before this evening, or else there *will* be trouble!"

Cyril Lightowler's shoulders drooped as he watched Gypsy Rosa rubbing at her crystal ball with a bright yellow duster. He had done everything that could reasonably be expected of him,

57

hadn't he? It wasn't his fault that the town was plagued with a vampire. And yet everything was against him. The police were being unco-operative. The local press and radio station were unfair. The town council would be sure to say he was to blame. And to cap it all, if he did not do something before the day was out, he would be in even deeper hot water with his wife. Suddenly he felt very angry.

"You're not getting anywhere, are you?" he snapped at the fortune-teller.

"I can't help it," replied Gypsy Rosa with a shrug. "It isn't as simple as looking at somebody's palm and telling them that they're going on a long journey. This is a sinister business. Vampires are hellish creatures. These are the Dark Impen-etrable Forces of Evil that we're dealing with now. It is a difficult task – even for the seventh daughter of the seventh daughter of a Ruritanian Romany princess—"

"Don't talk rubbish!" snarled the mayor as he leapt to his feet. "It's got nothing to do with the Dark Impenetrable Forces of Evil! You're just a rotten fortune-teller. You're not a real gypsy at all. And, what's more, you *know* that I know that you're not a real gypsy. Your name isn't Rosa. It's Edith Scroggins. We went to school together. Your father worked in a shoe shop and your mother used to play Bingo with my mother. So don't try and come that 'seventh daughter of a seventh daughter of a Ruritanian Romany prin-cess' gubbins with me!"

"Don't shout at me, Cyril Lightowler," said the fortune-teller, surprised at the mayor's anger. "If you feel like that, why did you come and see me in the first place?"

"For a bit of help," he growled. "Because I was fool enough to think that you might be able to see *something* in that silly crystal ball. But it's plainly obvious, Edith, that you can't see so much as a sausage!" With which, the mayor turned on his heel and swept out of the cubicle.

The bead curtain across the open doorway shook and rattled together for a couple of seconds and then there was silence.

"My goodness me! Somebody seems to have got out of the bed on the wrong side this morning," said Gypsy Rosa raising her eyebrows. "I wonder who's been getting up Cyril's nostrils?" She took a chocolate-covered toffee out of the bag she kept secreted on her lap, unwrapped it, popped it into her mouth and sucked it slowly, pondering on the cause of the mayor's anger.

"Have they caught that Dracula yet?" called the fat, rosy-cheeked lady as Scarcombe's mayor strode past her ice-cream stall.

But Cyril Lightowler, still smarting from his encounter with the fortune-teller, went on his way without so much as a glance. He had not heard. He was deep in thought. The mayor was trying to think of something he could say in his speech to his fellow town councillors that would excuse the fact that he had no good news for them regarding the capture of the vampire. He sucked in his cheeks as he tried to remember the fortune-teller's words. "A sinister business." "Hellish creatures." "The Dark Impenetrable Forces of Evil." Edith Scroggins had only been trying to flannel him, of course. All the same, they were impressive words. They were the sort of words that would sound even more impressive ringing round the echoing, vaulted, stone council chamber in Scarcombe's ancient town hall.

All at once, Cyril Lightowler's spirits rose. He knew what he was going to do. He would make a speech that was worthy of him, a speech to hold in thrall the entire council, friend and foe. With any luck, it would be published in full in that afternoon's edition of the *Evening Chronicle*. Dora, when she read it, might feel a little proud of him. Instead of snapping his head off when he got home, she might even cook his favourite toad-in-the-hole for supper that night.

The mayor of Scarcombe smirked a little smirk. He quickened his step. He was suddenly looking forward to the council meeting.

"Here, Igor! Here, Ivan! Come on, Olga! There's a good Babushka!" Assistant Zookeeper Granville Letchworth began to call out his greetings to the wolves long before he arrived at their compound – or "Spaciously Wooded Wolf Park" as it was optimistically described in the Wildlife Zoo's publicity leaflet. "Here, Rubka! Here, Relka! Come on, Lenin, you old rogue! Din-dins!"

At the sound of his voice, several of the younger wolves pulled themselves slowly to their feet and sauntered off, tongues lolling, towards the area of the wire mesh where they knew he would appear. The older wolves were in no hurry. They yawned and stretched before easing themselves up on to all four paws and padded off in pursuit of the others. There was plenty of time. They knew, from years of experience, that there would be sufficient dead meat for all of them. Never too little. Never too much. Just sufficient. Always the same amount exactly. Assistant Keeper Letchworth would have weighed it out to the last ounce in the food-preparation hut before setting out with his wheelbarrow. And there was never any squabbling over portions. The wolf pack had long since grown too bored and listless to consider arguing over which of them got what.

"Here, Mikhail! Come on, Tanya!" The assistant keeper had arrived at the selfsame spot outside the wire mesh where he turned up, at exactly the same time, every day of the year, pushing his barrow loaded with defrosted joints of meat. "Come on then, Kevin! Good girl, Tracey!" cried Granville Letchworth, lobbing hunks of meat, as if they were giant hand grenades, over the wire mesh.

It was not that the assistant keeper was afraid to enter the compound. The wolf pack had been in captivity for so long now that they would have taken the food out of his hand. But it was easier to toss the meat over the fence than go to the trouble of unlocking the rusting padlock on the gate.

"Good boy, Kevin! Good girl, Tracey! Eat up, my lovelies!" Granville Letchworth called out again to his two favourite charges. Kevin and Tracey were the only two wolves to have been born in the compound since he himself had been promoted to the post of Wolf Pack attendant, prior to which he had served his two obligatory years' probationary service in the dark, dank confines of the aquarium. The assistant keeper

had been allowed to choose the names of the two latest additions to the pack himself.

Inside the feeding area, the entire pack was gathered in a matter of moments, with each wolf either gnawing on a chunk of meat or whimpering softly, awaiting a turn at one of the joints.

The entire pack, that is, save one member.

Boris, the old leader, had still not made a move to join in the day's repast. He decided that he would join the others in his own good time. For the moment he was content to lie on his couch of pine needles, his nose resting on his outstretched front legs, staring without blinking at the man on the other side of the fence.

Boris did not like the assistant keeper. He despised the names that Letchworth had chosen for the youngest members of the pack. "Tracey" and "Kevin"! What sort of names were those to bestow upon two members of a wolf pack of Transylvanian descent? Admittedly, the two young wolves had known nothing but captivity and idleness, but there were such things as background and tradition.

These same troubled feelings had made him feel uneasy during the previous night. They had something to do with the night-time creature that had flitted silently through the moonlit treetops, and kindled in him the desire to plunge, unhindered, through mile after mile of thick, freshly fallen snow. He yearned to sniff the scent of quarry, to seek out a commanding mountain top, throw back his head, bare his fangs and howl at a silvery moon. He needed to experience freedom again. But how, as pack leader, could he keep this spirit of the wild alive among his followers, particularly when they answered to such unwolflike names as "Kevin" and "Tracey"?

Boris shook himself as he lurched to his feet. Lifting his right back leg, he scratched behind an ear where a particularly aggravating flea had recently taken up residence. He shook himself again and managed to shake off his worries. But as he padded down towards the feeding area, he knew that the problem had not gone away for ever – it was firmly in the back of his mind.

"Come along, Boris, you old slowcoach!" Assistant Zookeeper Granville Letchworth called out as the lean old wolf sidled out from the fringe of pine trees. "Didn't you hear me shouting? I don't know what we're going to do with you – I shall have to see about getting you a hearing aid, you silly old sausage!"

Boris shouldered his way past a couple of she-wolves and snatched up a half-eaten chunk of meat loosely attached to a tempting bone. He chewed on the meat reflectively. The old wolf knew that if he was to continue as leader of the pack, very soon he would need to assert that leadership.

5

Henry Hollins fingered a coin in his trouser pocket, gulped, took a deep breath and then made up his mind.

"One, please," he said, placing the coin on the well-worn brass counter inside the pay booth of the Ghost Train.

But the man inside, his face hidden behind his newspaper, was keenly studying the sports pages and either had not heard or was not interested in the boy's words. Henry sighed and then glanced idly around the amusement park as he waited for the man to acknowledge his presence.

Scarcombe's Popular Amusement Park wasn't particularly popular this morning with the town's holiday-makers. In fact, although it was very nearly eleven o'clock, the amusement park was almost deserted.

Henry totted up the sum total of visitors he could see inside the park. There were two men in shirtsleeves feeding coins into the one-armed bandits in the slot-machine arcade. A father and his young daughter were trying to throw table tennis balls into the tops of goldfish bowls at one of the circular side stalls. A young couple wandered arm in arm through the park, with eyes only for each other as they shared a stick of candy floss. There was a small boy, with his mother in attendance, sitting on a miniature steamroller and vigorously clanging its bell as he waited for the children's merry-go-round to start. That was only eight holiday-makers in the park. No, wait a minute, nine in all, counting himself.

"Yes, young feller-me-lad? And what can I do to oblige you?" The voice of the man behind the pay booth's counter broke in on Henry's thoughts. Reggie Perks had lowered his newspaper to reveal a cheery, round face and a head which was totally bald on top but with white tufts of hair sticking out above his ears.

"One, please," repeated Henry, again proffering Mr Perks his money.

"All aboard!" said Reggie, as he took the coin from Henry and indicated the Ghost Train's coaches standing in a row on their metal rails. They faced two wooden doors painted deep red in colour with a fearsome Frankenstein's monster face across them.

Henry crossed the wooden planking, took up his seat in the first of the coaches, pulled down the metal safety bar across his lap and settled himself as comfortably as possible on the hard wooden seat. Then, as he waited for the ride to begin, he chewed at his lower lip. Was he doing the right thing in taking a trip, all by himself, on the Scarcombe Ghost Train?

It was not that Henry Hollins was nervous at the prospect of encountering the ghouls, ghosties and other terrifying plywood creatures that lay in wait for him in the darkness on the other side of the double doors. Not a bit of it. He had ridden the Ghost Trains in amusement parks and fairs all over the country and had thoroughly enjoyed every hair-raising moment on each and every one of them. The idea of taking a trip on this one,

68

even by himself, did not cause him so much as a second's alarm. No, what was worrying Henry was whether he should be out enjoying himself when his friend, Count Alucard, might be somewhere in Scarcombe in dire need of his help. But what else could he possibly do to track down his Transylvanian chum?

Since breakfast, Henry had been scouring the promenade and shopping streets of the little seaside town in an attempt to discover some clue or hint that might assist him in his search for the Count. But, alas, without success. Indeed, there was nothing to suggest that Count Alucard had been anywhere in the region of Scarcombe. As the morning passed, the town had been quietly returning to normal. Those holiday-makers who had at first been frightened by the rumours of the vampire's presence, and had chosen to remain in the safety of their hotels and boarding houses, were now beginning to venture out of doors. Families were drifting down on to the sands, the adults carrying bulging beach bags and deck chairs, the children bearing buckets and spades and large inflatable toys. Henry's search had finally brought him to the amusement park and, strolling round the rides and sideshows, he found himself in front of the Ghost Train. It was only then that he decided to treat himself to a ride.

"Hold tight!" cried Reggie Perks, as he pressed a button which set the machinery in motion.

Henry Hollins felt a sudden jerk as his coach moved forward. Rumbling along the metal rails, the coach struck the two wooden doors, pushing them open, and then clattered through. As the doors swung shut behind him, Henry found himself in total darkness.

"*He-he-hee! Ha-ha-haa! Hoo-hoo-hooOOOO!*" An eerie laugh echoed in the blackness and then something brushed lightly over Henry's face.

But Henry Hollins wasn't at all spooked by any of this. He had travelled too often on Ghost Trains to be put off by such minor incidents. He knew that the ghostly laughter came from a recording which was triggered by the movement of his coach. He also knew that the spidery thing that had softly stroked his cheek was nothing more than a piece of string, dangling somewhere overhead.

The coach lurched as it took a sudden sharp turn to the right, tossing Henry into a corner, and a glowing green witch with a hooked nose and a pointed chin rose up on a broomstick on his left and swooped across the track in front of him.

"*He-he-heee! Ha-ha-haaa! Hoo-hoo-hooOOOO!*" The ghostly laughter rang out again but, this time, from somewhere closer at hand.

Henry Hollins shifted into the centre of his seat and took a firm grip on the safety rail as the coach rattled onwards. First red, then green, then orange lights flashed on and off. He was hurtling into a solid brick wall directly in the coach's path. Henry gulped and waited for the inevitable crash but, just before the moment of impact, the wall swung outwards on either side of the coach and,

simultaneously, a grinning skeleton appeared, rattling its bones as it shot upwards and out of sight.

"*He-he-heee! Ha-ha-haaa! Hoo-hoo-hooOOOO!*"

And now a red-faced, two-horned, grinning
devil lunged with a sharp-pronged golden trident
as the coach took a sudden, unexpected turn to
the left – and brought Henry face to face with an
Egyptian mummy which leant out of its sarcophagus and waved arms encased in flapping, rotting
bandages.

The coach was travelling at breakneck speed,
forcing Henry to cling grimly on to the safety rail
with both his hands. His breath was held and his
eyes were open wide as the coach sped on and on,
banking sharply as one turn followed hard on
another. Now to the left. Now to the right. Now
to the left again. Monster after monster swung out
from either side, or rose up from out of nowhere,
or dropped down on him from above and, on each
of these occasions, missed him by the merest
fraction of an inch.

Henry guessed that the ride could not have long
to go. For Ghost Train rides, as everyone knows,
although jampacked tight with incidents, are over
almost before they have begun. Henry was just
starting to relax. He looked ahead for that crack
of daylight which would announce the exit. At
that moment, when he was least expecting a
surprise, the Ghost Train presented him with its
biggest surprise of all.

In the distance appeared a grey-green glow
lighting up a burial scene complete with a head-

stone, a wreath of lilies and an open grave. Then, as the coach hurtled closer towards this eerie scene, a figure arose from the grave.

"*He-he-heee! Ha-ha-haaa! Hoo-hoo-hooOOOO!*"

The figure was wearing a black suit and a starched white shirt with a black bow tie. It had a gold medallion on a chain round its neck and, over its shoulders was draped a scarlet-lined black cloak. It had a pale, drawn face, with dark, enquiring eyes and a black mane of hair which was swept back smoothly from its high forehead. Most surprising of all, though, was that this figure did not appear to be fashioned from wood, or *papier maché* or wax, like the other creatures. This figure seemed to be made of flesh and blood.

"Whooo-hooooOOOOH!" went the figure.

"Count Alucard!" yelled Henry Hollins.

But he called out the name too late, for his coach had already passed the graveyard tableau and was heading towards a crack of daylight up ahead.

"And in answer to Councillor Corcoran's question . . ." began the mayor, pausing to smooth down the ermine facing on his crimson robes, while he glanced round the packed council chamber before continuing: " . . . I would merely point out to him that our gallant police force are doing a grand job in their efforts to apprehend the vampire."

The councillors belonging to the same political party as the mayor made polite noises to show that they were in full agreement with him. At the same time, the town councillors who were on the other side of the political fence made impolite noises to indicate that they did not agree at all with what he was saying.

"In fact," the mayor went on, "I'd say that the town's policemen were doing a fantastic job."

"Hear, hear," mumbled his political partners.

But their words were drowned in a storm of angry cries from his opponents: "Rubbish!" they called, and, "Shame!" and, "Speak up, Cyril – we can't hear you at the back!" and, even, "Resign, resign!"

"Perhaps the mayor might care to tell us then," said Councillor Colin Corcoran, a tall thin man with a hooked nose, taking advantage of the hubbub to get on to his feet again, "why the police station was closed at nine o'clock this morning with a note for the milkman pinned to the door?"

Scarcombe's mayor took out a clean, folded, blue-bordered white hanky from his trouser pocket and dabbed at the beads of perspiration on his forehead. Cyril Lightowler was apt to perspire quite a lot and things were not going well for him so far in the council chamber. Never mind, he still had one or two aces up his sleeve in the shape of the fortune-teller's splendid phrases. It would not be long before he brought them into play.

"I don't know how much my fellow councillor knows or, perhaps, does not know, about the lifestyle of vampires," the mayor replied, with an edge of sarcasm creeping into his voice. "But I would just point out to him that he would hardly be likely to come across Count Dracula in the Mermaid Fish and Chip shop, in broad daylight, asking for a portion of haddock and chips with salt and vinegar!"

"I fail to see wh-wh-what fish-and-chips have got to do with—" stammered Councillor Corcoran who, as well as being one of the mayor's chief political enemies, was also the owner of the Mermaid Fish and Chip Café. But his words were cut short by cackles of glee from Cyril Lightowler's supporters.

"Ha-ha-haaa!" and "He-he-hee!" they chortled, enjoying Corcoran's embarrassment.

"Vampires are, by nature, creatures of darkness," the mayor continued, pressing home his advantage. "Which is precisely why our brave police force was out all night looking for the owner of that fearful coffin."

"Hear, hear!" cried his supporters, while his adversaries held their silence, knowing that the mayor was coming off best in the argument.

"The apprehending of vampires is a sinister

business," continued the mayor, having decided that the time was ripe to use the best bits of the speech which he had been holding back. "Vampires are hellish creatures. What the town is being asked to deal with here are the Dark Impenetrable Forces of Evil!"

Cyril Lightowler paused again. This time his words were greeted with absolute silence. He knew that, at that moment, he held the entire council in the palm of his hand. He had been right in thinking that the fortune-teller's words would have a striking effect in the council chamber. They had sounded awesomely chilling as they had echoed around the ancient vaulted walls. Out of the corner of his eye, he could see into the press box where the *Evening Chronicle*'s ace reporter, Royston Renshaw, was hard at work taking down his every word.

"Be assured, though, that the vampire – or vampires, if there be more than one – will never gain the upper hand in good old Scarcombe," the mayor continued and then paused, not knowing what to say next.

The trouble was that he had used up all of the fortune-teller's exciting phrases. Here he stood, on the threshold of the best speech he had ever made in his life and he was lost for words. Cyril Lightowler racked his brains. Suddenly he remembered something that he had read once in a book of famous speeches and which, with a little alteration, might just suit the occasion.

"We shall fight them on the beaches," the

mayor continued, pinching some wartime words of Winston Churchill. "We shall fight them in the fields and in the streets. We shall fight them on the cliffs. We shall never surrender!"

Scarcombe's town council rose, cheered, whistled through their fingers and stamped their feet. In the press box, Renshaw's ballpoint pen was fairly flying across the pages of his notebook.

From the shelter of the goldfish side stall, Henry Hollins watched as the Ghost Train attendant folded up his newspaper, stuck it in his jacket pocket, placed a BACK IN 15 MINUTES sign in the pay-booth window, and then strolled off towards the entrance to the amusement park. Once the man was out of sight, Henry darted across, mounted the steps to the Ghost Train platform, then tiptoed past the line of motionless coaches towards the entrance. Placing both hands on the Frankenstein monster's face which was painted across the red double doors, Henry pushed, hard. The doors swung silently open and, as Henry stepped inside, silently closed behind him. Henry gulped and swallowed. Standing in the dark, still, silent Ghost Train proved a much more scary experience than the ride which he had taken in the comfort of the coach and to the reassuring sound of the recorded ghostly laughter.

"Count Alucard!" cried Henry, into the blackness which stretched before him. He had intended to call out loudly and clearly but the sound that had come out of his mouth was a croaking hiss. Henry Hollins cleared his throat and tried again. "Count Alucard! It's *me*! Henry Hollins!" He paused, and listened hard, but there was nothing to be heard. "There's nothing to be afraid of, Count! Surely you remember me? I came to your castle in Transylvania. Henry Hollins! I'm your *friend*!"

There were several moments of silence, then Henry thought he heard a movement.

"Henry Hollins?" The voice that called out to him sounded even more nervous than his own. "Is it really you?"

"*Yes!*" Henry tried to make his voice seem firm and reassuring. "I rode round on the Ghost Train about an hour ago. I recognised you coming up out of that coffin. There's nobody here with me, Count. It's quite safe. I'm on my own. *Honestly!*"

There were several more moments of silence, except for a rustle in the darkness, and then the voice spoke in his ear.

"Hello, Henry."

It made Henry jump, not because he was frightened – just startled by the sudden close proximity of the vegetarian vampire Count.

"*Goodness*! Am I pleased to see you, Henry!" Count Alucard continued. "That is to say, I *shall* be pleased, as soon as I can see you properly – it's so *dark* in here!"

Henry put out his hand and touched the Count's flowing robe.

"Here," said Henry. "Put your hand on my

shoulder while I take a peep outside." As soon as he felt Count Alucard's long, thin fingers on his collar, Henry turned and pushed open the double doors just far enough to be able to peer out through the crack into the amusement park. "There's nobody close by," he said. "It's safe for us to go outside – if we sit in the front coach, no one can see us."

"Are you *absolutely* sure of that?"

"Positive," said Henry. "There's a sign up saying that the Ghost Train's closed for quarter of an hour. And the man who runs the ride only went off a couple of minutes ago – we'll be quite safe for the next ten minutes at least."

"Well, if you say so, Henry, I believe you," said Count Alucard. "You lead the way."

Henry Hollins slipped out through the double doors and the Count came after him, his long, pale hand still resting on the boy's shoulder. Henry led the way into the Ghost Train's front coach.

"Wow!" said Count Alucard, letting out a sigh of relief and flopping down next to Henry. "Am I glad to take a break. It's as black as pitch in there. And ever so spooky!"

"I thought you could see in the dark?"

"Only when I turn into a bat," the Count replied. "And I can only do that when it's night-time."

"How did you get inside there in the first place?" asked Henry.

"Oh, it's all official and very much above board,

Henry, I assure you," said the Count, fluttering his fingers in the air. "It's my job. I work here. I was *very* lucky really. Would you care to hear about it?"

"Yes, please," said Henry Hollins and, as he spoke, he dug his hand into a jacket pocket and took out a round rosy fruit, adding: "But, first of all, would you like to have this?"

"Why, it's a peach!" cried Count Alucard, his dark eyes flashing with delight.

"Mmmm." Henry nodded his head. "I bought it in a fruit shop just off the promenade. I've been looking all over Scarcombe for you. I guessed, if I did find you, you might be hungry."

"I'm absolutely famished, as a matter of fact. You *are* thoughtful." Count Alucard sank his sharp, shiny-white pointed teeth into the juicy golden flesh. "Oh! Sheer ecstasy!" he murmured. There were several moments of silence while he chewed, with obvious deep pleasure, on his first mouthful of peach. He swallowed it and let out a long, slow sigh of satisfaction. "My word, Henry, that *is* good!"

"Finish it off," urged Henry.

"No, thank you. Not just now. I'll take it back in there with me and eat it later," said Count Alucard. He flicked a black silk handkerchief from out of his top pocket, spread it out on the wooden seat and placed the part-eaten peach in the centre. "We haven't got a great deal of time and there is *so* much that I have to tell you."

"What are you doing here in Scarcombe? And what's been happening to you since we last met? Did you ever get your castle back after those peasants ransacked it? How long have you been working on the Ghost Train—"

"Please, Henry, *please!*" exclaimed the Count, throwing up his hands in mock horror and cutting his young friend short. "Taking your last question first, though, I only got the Ghost Train job this morning. I was *so* lucky! I'd climbed over the fence into the amusement park from the ornamental gardens. It was still quite early and there was hardly anyone about. I was looking for a hiding place. Well, you'll hardly believe this, Henry, but I was standing over there . . ." He paused to flap a pale and bony hand towards the concreted area in front of the Ghost Train, and then continued: "There was a sign in front of the pay booth saying 'Man Wanted'. The job was for a chap to bob up and down in the coffin when the coaches rattle past, pretending to be Dracula. Mr Perks thought I was someone looking for the job – bringing my own costume with me, so to speak! Wasn't that an incredible coincidence?"

"It certainly was, Count," Henry agreed. "But all the other monsters in the Ghost Train aren't *real* people, are they? Surely they're all made from metal and wood?"

"Oh, they are, they are! You don't imagine for one moment that I'd hang about in the dark if they were *real* monsters, do you? My goodness me, Henry, you wouldn't see the back of my cloak for dust! It's spooky enough inside that Ghost Train as it is! No, the Dracula that's usually in the coffin – the one that's made of metal and wood – has had to go away to be repaired. I've only got the job until that one comes back. Mine's just a temporary position."

"Didn't Mr Perks recognise you? Hadn't he read about you in the newspaper? Hadn't it occurred to him, when he saw you, that you could be the *real* Count Dracula?"

"Not for a second." Count Alucard shook his head and his long black hair swayed from side to side at the back of his head. "He only ever reads the sports pages. I'm willing to have a wager with you that he is at the bookmaker's right now, having a bet on a horse race. And, speaking of Mr Perks, Henry, I really ought to be getting inside that coffin again before he comes back." As he spoke, Count Alucard gathered up the four corners of the black silk handkerchief, enclosing the part-eaten peach neatly within the folds.

"Yes, I suppose you should," said Henry, glumly. "But what are you going to do about things? Where are you going to go tonight after you finish here? They've had the town's entire police force out looking for you!"

"Mmm," replied the Count, shrugging in a sad sort of way, his shoulders drooping underneath his cloak. "I don't know why they can't just leave me alone. It isn't as if I've done anything wrong. It's just because of who I am – or who my forebears were. Good heavens above, *I* don't go around biting people's necks. I wouldn't dream of doing such a thing." And, as if to prove the point, he gave a little shudder of distaste.

"I know," said Henry, smiling sympathetically at the Count who was beginning to look rather tired and more than a little sorry for himself. "Can't you move on somewhere else?"

"Not until I've got *my* coffin back," Count Alucard's voice rose indignantly. "And I don't even know what they've done with that. They hadn't any right to take it away from me. It's stealing. It's my personal private property. I'm absolutely lost without it. I can't get a good night's sleep without that coffin. It's all very well turning myself into a bat at night, but I don't get my *proper* sleep. It's extremely uncomfortable hanging upside down. Those policemen should be made to try it."

"What time does the amusement park close for the night?" asked Henry briskly. He felt that it was time to change the subject before the Count got totally wrapped up in self pity.

"Just after dark. About half past nine."

"Why don't you and I meet somewhere about ten o'clock tonight then?"

"Could we *really*, Henry?" asked Count Alucard, cheering up immediately at being given the chance of seeing Henry again.

"I don't see why not. I'm sure I could manage to slip away for a little while. Mum and Dad are going to see the Talent Contest in the Recreational Hall tonight. Do you know the Caravan Leisure Park on top of the cliffs?"

"I'm sure I could find it."

"It's close to the Wildlife Zoo Park."

"Oh, I know where that is – I swooped over it last night while I was being a bat."

"Good. I'll meet you by the wire fence between the zoo and the leisure park," said Henry. "Behind the swimming-pool changing huts. Ten o'clock sharp."

"I'll be there," replied the Count.

"I'll try and get you some more fruit."

"I'd be awfully grateful, if it isn't too much trouble for you. And now, I really *must* be getting back." Count Alucard was beginning to sound like his old cheerful self again. "I'm so looking forward to finishing off this peach inside that plywood coffin. You never know, Henry – if I can keep clear of trouble long enough for them to realise that I don't go round nipping people on their necks, they might change their minds about me, don't you think?"

"They might, Count," said Henry Hollins, giving his friend an encouraging smile.

"Jolly good!" replied the Count. "Ten o'clock, then. Sharp." With which he moved off along the Ghost Train's track, pushing his way through the red double doors.

But the moment Count Alucard was out of sight, the smile faded from Henry's face and it was his turn to look sad. "They *might* change their minds about you, Count," he said softly to himself, "but I wouldn't like to bet on it."

It was at this point exactly that he caught a glimpse of Mr Perks crossing the amusement park on his way back to the Ghost Train. Luckily for Henry, the Ghost Train's attendant had his face buried, as usual, inside the sports pages of his newspaper. Henry Hollins was able to get down from the Ghost Train's coach, unseen by Mr Perks, and slip quietly away through the rides and stalls and sideshows.

6

TOWN TERRORISED BY DARK EVIL FORCES!

It screamed, in enormous black letters across the top of the front page of Scarcombe's *Evening Chronicle* that afternoon. And underneath, in letters that were only slightly smaller, was printed the sub-heading:

FEARLESS MAYOR PLEDGES "NO SURRENDER"!

Dora Lightowler wriggled herself into a more comfortable position on the flower-patterned sofa, folded the newspaper in half, and began to read Royston Renshaw's article:

Scarcombe's historic council chamber echoed to many a brave word today when the town's mayor, Councillor Cyril Lightowler, delivered a stirring speech which was almost worthy of this country's great wartime leader, Winston Churchill. Referring to the gang of blood-drinking vampires at present preying on Scarcombe's population – men, women and children alike – and reported to be reaching plague proportions, the mayor gave the council his solemn assurance that the evil creatures would be shown no mercy. The council members thronging the ancient chamber rose to their feet and cheered as Cyril Lightowler spoke out on behalf of Scarcombe's innocent victims of the Dark Impenetrable Forces of Evil—

"My word, Cyril," began Dora Lightowler, "it makes me feel quite proud of you! I wish I'd been in the council chamber to hear your speech."

Cyril Lightowler shrugged modestly as if to suggest that stirring speeches tripped off his tongue quite regularly. "It did go down rather well, Dora," he said. "How was your day, dear? How were things at the Glamorous Granny competition on the pier?"

"That seemed to go down rather well too, Cyril," Dora replied with a smile. "It was won by a sixty-five-year-old lady with blonde hair wearing a Hawaiian grass skirt. There's a picture of me on page five presenting her with the First Prize: a plastic lemonade jug and six matching tumblers."

"Well done, Dora," observed Cyril, turning to the relevant page in the copy of that afternoon's newspaper.

The Lightowlers had a standing arrangement with their newsagent: whenever either of them was mentioned in the pages of their local newspaper, the paper boy was to deliver two copies instead of the usual one. They clipped the pertinent article out of the first copy and stuck it in a scrapbook they were keeping; the second copy was posted off to Cyril's mother, Florence Lightowler, a white-haired old lady who lived in a senior citizens' sheltered accommodation block of flats in Grange-over-Sands. This particular year, when Cyril and Dora were fulfilling the roles of Scarcombe's mayor and mayoress, meant particularly expensive newsagent's bills.

"Cyril, dear?" began Dora, "is this vampire business really getting out of hand?"

"Rest assured, Dora, that our gallant police force will be able to cope with it. Arrests are pending. By the way, dear, what are we having for supper?"

"Your favourite, Cyril. Toad-in-the-hole," replied Mrs Lightowler.

Scarcombe's mayor licked his lips in anticipation of that treat as he studied the photograph of his wife in her mayoress's regalia, presenting the plastic prize to a rather elderly looking lady wearing a Hawaiian grass skirt and a bikini top.

Peace, harmony and a general air of well-being reigned over the mayoral household. In times to come, though, the Lightowlers would look back on those moments as the calm before the storm.

"I give up," said Police Constable Woolley, with a puzzled shake of his head.

"Don't give up yet, Norman," urged his companion, Police Constable Barncastle. "Try again. Just one more time."

PC Woolley screwed up his eyes, pushed his helmet to the back of his head, put his face close up to the glass and peered hard into the window of the seafront gift shop on the end of the promenade. "Errr . . . is it C for coasters, Barry?" he asked his fellow policeman.

"You what?" replied Barncastle. "Coasters? What's them when they're at home?"

"You know! Those little round things made of raffia," said Woolley, pointing into the window with his truncheon. "You put them underneath your glass when you're having a drink of anything. They're to stop your glass making little round stains on the polished furniture."

"Oh, *those*!" said Constable Barncastle. "We've got some at our house. Only ours aren't made of raffia, they're plastic with pictures of fox-hunting scenes on them. My mum goes spare if I forget to use them." He glanced admiringly at Woolley. "I never knew they were called 'coasters', though. Thanks for telling me."

"Don't mention it," said Norman Woolley. "But, I'll tell you what – you can do me a favour in return. You can tell me what it is you've Spied With Your Little Eye Beginning with C."

"Comb-case."

"Where?"

"Over there, numbskull!" It was Barry Barncastle's turn to take out his truncheon and point into the shop window. "Use your eyes, Norman. There's three of them. Behind those key-rings. They're red leatherette and they've got the Scarcombe coat of arms on them. You're a copper. You're supposed to be observant."

"Oh, *them*! I must need glasses. I thought they were bookmarks." Norman Woolley stuck his truncheon back into its holder and looked along the seafront. He'd had enough of "I-Spy With My Little Eye" for the time being. "Fancy a stroll along the prom, Barry?"

"Suits me, Norman."

The two policemen crossed over the road and set off, in jaunty mood, along the iron-railinged promenade. It was 8.30 p.m. precisely (or "twenty thirty hours" in police parlance) and a restful hour, at that time of year, between daylight and dark. And, although they both knew that another long night's duty lay ahead, with a vampire still on the loose, neither of them minded one little bit. For, unlike the previous night when Scarcombe's policemen had been called upon to search single-handed, tonight their orders from Station Sergeant Downend were to patrol the town and its surroundings in pairs.

"I'm glad we're going out in twos tonight, Barry, instead of patrolling on our own," Constable Woolley confided to his companion, as they moved along the promenade side by side and stride for stride.

"Me too, Norman!" enthused PC Barncastle.

If anything, it was probable that Barry Barncastle was more grateful for that circumstance than his partner. Barncastle had not yet plucked up sufficient courage to tell his station sergeant that he had lost his torch during the previous night's duty. The possibility of his being sent out on duty alone, and with nothing to light up the town's dark alleys and shadowy corners, had been troubling him all day. He had lost sleep over it. But now everything was all right. Not only did he have a companion to share the midnight hours, but his companion carried a torch tucked in at his belt. Constable Barncastle felt doubly relieved.

"Shall we try a toddle round the amusement park, Barry?" asked Constable Woolley, as the bright lights of the rides and sideshows hove into view and the evening drifted into darkness.

"Do you think we should?" asked Constable Barncastle doubtfully. "We weren't told to include the amusement park in our beat, were we?"

"No, but we weren't told not to either, Barry," replied Woolley, who was the slightly more adventurous of the pair. "Our instructions were to keep our eyes skinned for vampires. We're just as likely to spot them in the amusement park as out of it – *more* likely, in fact," he reasoned, "it's not as dark in there as it is outside."

There is, as the old saying goes, many a true word spoken in jest.

"Who were you with last night,
Out in the pale moonlight . . .?"

"I've seen that woman somewhere before," hissed Albert Hollins, leaning across and whispering into the ear of his wife, Emily, and nodding up at the elderly lady with the blonde hair, wearing a grass

skirt and a bikini top, who was singing into the microphone on the stage of the Caravan Leisure Park's Recreational Hall.

> "It wasn't your brother,
> It wasn't your ma . . ."

"Of course you have, Albert," Emily hissed back. "She won that lemonade jug and those glasses on the pier this afternoon."

It was true. The elderly lady, flushed with success at having won the First Prize in the Glamorous Granny competition, had decided to push her luck by entering the Talent Contest that same evening.

> "Oh, oh, oh,
> And it wasn't your pa . . .!

"Come on, everybody!" entreated the elderly lady. "Altogether now! One more time!"

Dutifully, the holiday-makers in the recreational hall joined in half-heartedly as the elderly lady burst into a second chorus of the music hall song, at the same time conducting with her hands to encourage the audience.

"She isn't much good, is she?" whispered Albert. "She might have won the lemonade jug and the half-dozen glasses, but I can't see her picking up the First Prize at tonight's shindig."

"What is the First Prize?" asked Emily, without much interest, her mind on other things.

"Why, it's that blue and red teddy bear over there, isn't it?" asked Albert, indicating a hideous cuddly toy which was standing on a table at the side of the hall, propped up against the Second Prize: a large bottle of bubble bath tied up with a red ribbon.

"I suppose it must be," Emily replied and then, without pausing, she continued: "I do hope our Henry's all right in that caravan on his own."

"Of course Henry's okay," said Albert Hollins reassuringly. "He *wanted* to be on his own tonight.

You heard him say so. There's a programme he wants to watch on the telly. He's as safe as houses inside that caravan."

"I know," sighed Emily. "It's just that with all this talk of vampires in the newspaper . . ."

"*Newspapers!*" said Albert, scornfully. "You don't want to believe what they tell you. What did it say in the newspaper horoscope on my birthday? That I was going to go on a long journey. And what happened to me in real life? I sprained my ankle walking down the garden path and I couldn't get out of the house for a fortnight. *Newspapers*! Huh, if you ask me—"

Albert broke off to join in half-heartedly with the audience as they applauded the elderly lady who, having finished her song, gave them a "twirl" in her grass skirt and skipped gaily off the stage.

"All the same—" began Emily.

"Ssshhhh!" hissed Albert. "Here comes the next contestant."

Emily, deciding that Albert was probably right and that she was worrying unduly, settled back in her seat as the next contestant, a man wearing a red false nose and a lampshade on his head, began to juggle with two oranges and an apple.

Henry Hollins, crouched behind the swimming-pool's changing rooms, held his breath as he listened to the soft whimpering sounds that were coming from the wolf pack on the other side of the wire-mesh fence.

On the previous night, after the first shock at hearing their cries, Henry Hollins had lain in his bed drifting in and out of sleep to the howling of the wolves. The sounds had not worried him one little bit. But these urgent, restless, fretful whimperings were more unnerving. Besides, on the night before he had been secure in the knowledge that his mother and father were close at hand. Tonight he was all alone, out of doors, and with a night wind soughing in the tall treetops.

Henry lifted his hand and pointed his watch at the moon, screwing up his eyes as he tried to make out the time. Half past nine. Was that all? Half an hour to go before Count Alucard was due to arrive. In his eagerness to see his friend, Henry had set out *much* too early.

He patted both his jacket pockets to make sure that the half-pound of plums were all whole and safe, then settled himself down in the grass and waited for the minutes to pass. Coming from a long way off was the sound of the music from the amusement park rides, rising and falling on the wind. The park hadn't yet closed down for the night. Henry shivered and drew his collar up round his ears as the whimpering started up again. Boris, the wily old pack leader, padded in and around the wolves herded together for comfort and protection. It was the younger wolves that were doing the whimpering. Igor and Olga trembled, with saliva dripping from their lower jaws. Kevin and Tracey both panted fast and made each other more and more nervous.

Boris was half-inclined to give these younger wolves a warning nip across their flanks to stop them whining – except that another part of him sympathised with the young wolves' anxieties. For the wolf pack leader was also experiencing an animal sixth sense that warned him that something strange was going to happen before the night was through.

So instead of nipping the younger wolves with his fangs, Boris satisfied himself by growling in warning at Igor and Kevin, then comfortingly nuzzled Olga and Tracey, calming all their fears. Boris knew that together the pack is as strong as its leader; divided it's as weak as the youngest cub. Whatever it was that had to be faced that night, the wolves would face up to it together.

"If you're really interested, Barry," said Constable Woolley, as the two policemen strolled through the gaily lit stalls and sideshows in the amusement park, "you want to come down to the Market Hall any Wednesday night and have a try yourself."

"I don't think I'd be much good at Formation Team Dancing, Norman," replied Constable Barncastle, shaking his head and glancing down at his size eleven policeman's boots which contained his size eleven feet.

"You don't know what you can do, or what you can't do, until you try," advised Woolley. "I never thought I'd get the hang of it when I first started – but you should see me now. Watch this!" As he spoke, Police Constable Woolley rose up on to the toes of his own well-polished, large-sized policeman's boots and, taking an imaginary female partner round the waist, performed a tricky sequence of formation dance steps across a quiet corner of the emptying amusement park. He ended his display by executing a neat pirouette before sliding down on to one knee. As he did so, his helmet slipped forward over his eyes.

"Great, Norman!" enthused Barncastle. "That was really smart!"

"Dead easy – when you know how," said Norman Woolley with a modest shrug, his arms outstretched, and with one knee still on the ground.

But the constable's dance steps had not gone unobserved. The man who owned the children's merry-go-round paused in the act of shrouding his ride with its plastic sheeting and watched the uniformed constable's dance steps in wide-eyed disbelief. He stood frozen, staring open-mouthed at the kneeling Woolley.

"I must have skidded on a banana skin or something," said Norman Woolley, as he got to his feet and gave the merry-go-round man an embarrassed grin. Then, turning back to Barncastle who was trying to hide a smile, he continued quickly, and out of the corner of his mouth: "Come on! Let's get away from here double quick! This way!" he hissed, moving up the wooden ramp which led to the nearest ride.

Reggie Perks, behind the counter of the Ghost Train's pay booth, looked over the top of the sports pages of that evening's *Chronicle* as the two policemen approached him.

"Two, please," said Norman Woolley, feeling for his money in the pockets of his navy-blue serge trousers.

A moment later, the two policemen were sitting in the front carriage on the Ghost Train, waiting for the ride to begin.

"Norman?" said Barry Barncastle nervously, clutching tight with both hands to the safety rail as he contemplated the fearsome painting of Frankenstein's monster on the red double doors.

"What?"

"Do you think it's going to be scary?"

"Who cares?" replied Constable Woolley, carelessly, trying to sound a little braver than he really felt.

The carriage containing the two policemen jolted as the attendant pressed the switch, and then rumbled forward, in fits and starts, along the track towards the wooden double doors.

7

"He-he-heee! Ha-ha-haaa! Hoo-hoo-hooOOO!"

The eerie laughter rang out in the Ghost Train as the coach, containing Constables Barncastle and Woolley, rattled into the pitch black darkness.

"Oooh-er! Mother!" yelled Barry Barncastle as something spidery brushed across his face.

"Get off me, Barry!" chortled Norman Woolley as the coach took a sudden turn to the right. He was thrown into a corner with his companion wedged up tight beside him. Red, green, then orange lights flashed ahead of them and Constable Barncastle tried to shift his weight across the seat and back into the upright position.

"He-he-heee! Ha-ha-haaa! Hoo-hoo-hooOOO!"

Again, the spooky laughter echoed in the darkness and the two policemen clung on to the coach's safety rail with all four of their hands.

"Look out!" screamed Barry Barncastle as the seemingly solid brick wall was suddenly illuminated ahead of them and he almost banged his head as he tried to duck below the level of the front of the coach.

"Oh, help!" yelled Norman Woolley, frozen with fear and staring in horror as the coach hurtled towards the wall.

Then, when the wall swung outwards on either side of them just before the moment of impact, the two policemen grabbed each other as the grinning skeleton rattled its bones, shot upwards and disappeared somewhere over their heads.

"Flippin' hummers!" gasped Constable Barncastle.

"Fizzin' heckers!" groaned Constable Woolley.

But the two policemen, sitting side by side, their arms outstretched, their knuckles showing white as they held on tightly to the safety rail, had scarcely recovered from their encounter with the rattling skeleton when they were next faced with the red-faced, two-horned, grinning devil lunging at them with its golden trident.

"Blimey O'Reilly!" wailed Woolley.

"Crickey Moses!" sobbed Barncastle.

Then, as they swept past the grinning devil, which was swallowed up in the tunnel behind them, the policemen gulped with fright as the gruesome mummy loomed up ahead, leaning out of its sarcophagus and waving its rotting bandages in their faces.

"No more, no more!" cried Barncastle.

"Let me out of here!" shouted Woolley.

The Ghost Train coach raced onwards, picking up speed as it rattled round one bend after another, with each turn bringing a new kind of spooky monster. And now the shrieks and screams of the coach's occupants were mingled with their nervous laughter for, truth to tell, they were beginning to enjoy being thoroughly frightened.

"Oh, lumme!" giggled Woolley, as the coach sped round yet another bend where, this time, a werewolf bared its slobbering jaws at them while its eyes glowed a scary green. "Shall we stop on after it's over, Barry, and go round again?"

"Why not, Norman?" chuckled Barncastle. "I can stand it if you can!"

But the Ghost Train held a secret in store for the two policemen that was to come as a bigger surprise than anything that had gone before. Several bends ahead, Count Alucard lay in his plywood coffin and prepared himself for the arrival of the oncoming coach.

It had not been a particularly busy afternoon and evening on the Ghost Train. Those holiday-makers that had not been scared out of Scarcombe by the talk of vampires in the town had certainly read or heard enough about the creatures not to want to meet similar monsters on the amusement park's spooky ride.

The vampire Count, therefore, had enjoyed a reasonably relaxing day. Since his meeting that morning with Henry Hollins, the vegetarian vampire had spent most of his time relaxing in the peace and comfort of his imitation coffin. He had been called upon no more than a dozen times to leap up, flap his cloak, flash his fangs and scream out "Whooo-hooooOOOOH!" at the occupants of the passing coaches. He guessed that his day's work was almost over. The coach approaching now was probably the last he would have to deal with before the ride closed down for the night.

Count Alucard decided to give the occupants of this last ride his very best shot. He gripped the hem of his cloak with his long, pale fingers then, as he heard the metal wheels of the coach spin round the final bend, he braced himself for a really scary final performance.

Barncastle and Woolley were just beginning to relax. Believing that the Ghost Train could have little more to offer them in the way of shocks, they had begun to loosen their hold on the coach's safety rail. They exchanged a reassuring grin as the train approached the open grave with its wreath of lilies, lit by the grey-green glow.

"Get ready for this one, Barry!" cried Constable Woolley, as the graveyard tableau hurtled towards them.

Suddenly, a black-cloaked figure leapt out of the grave.

"Whooo-hoo—" began Count Alucard, but his unearthly cry was cut short in his throat.

"Ooooohh—" began Constable Barncastle, but his anticipatory joyful scream ended almost before it had begun.

It was difficult to work out which of the three of them was most frightened by the encounter. Count Alucard, who had leapt up out of the grave to find two policemen bearing down on him – or the policemen themselves who had expected a cardboard monster but had found themselves staring at a vampire Count made of flesh and blood.

If the Count had continued with his scream the two constables might have been fooled into thinking that he was just one more cardboard creation. But Count Alucard could hardly be blamed for not having reacted quickly enough. After all, the last thing he had expected to come across inside the Ghost Train was a pair of policemen. The instant he had caught sight of them he dropped all pretence at being a fairground monster and simply stood and stared in horror and disbelief.

For their part, Barncastle and Woolley were equally aghast at coming face to face with the vampire. Although they had been detailed to find him, they had certainly not expected to encounter him inside the Ghost Train.

Everything, of course, was over in a couple of seconds. One moment, the policemen had been hurtling towards the Count in the speeding coach – a moment later the coach had carried them past. And, only a couple of moments after that, the two constables found themselves sitting in a stationary coach on the platform outside the ride's exit doors.

"We didn't imagine it, did we, Norman?" asked Constable Barncastle, searching his companion's face for confirmation of the vision. "It was Count Dracula we rode past in there?"

"It was him all right, Barry," replied Woolley, nodding his head solemnly. "You couldn't mistake him: long black cloak; pointy teeth; bloodshot starey eyes – the lot! Oh, yes – it was Dracula all right!"

The two policemen remained exactly where they

were, sitting in the coach which was now positioned at the back of the line, pondering over their lucky escape.

"He could have bitten us, Norman," said Constable Barncastle, aghast. "He could have stuck those two long pointy teeth into our necks – and then where would we have been? We'd have turned into vampires ourselves, you know."

Norman Woolley nodded slowly and then, galvanised into action, grabbed his small two-way radio on his uniform jacket. He flicked the "On" switch. "Charlie Bravo here," he said. "Charlie Bravo calling Fox Leader. Over."

Count Alucard crept slowly out of the open grave and along the pitch black twists and turns of the track. He had to find another hiding place before the policemen returned. But where? He couldn't stay inside the Ghost Train, for they would surely be coming to look for him. But it would be foolish to steal outside because they would be waiting there to arrest him. But he'd have to make a break for it before they called up reinforcements. On top of all that, he had promised to meet Henry Hollins up on the cliff top. Henry was the only person in Scarcombe – possibly the only person in the entire world – whom he could call his friend. Yes, he would certainly have to run for it. But not just yet . . .

"We've got him, Mr Mayor! Bingo!" said Police Sergeant Downend, excitedly flicking off the station's radio. "He's trapped inside the Ghost Train!"

"Is it just the one vampire then?" asked Cyril Lightowler, who was beginning to wonder if he hadn't got a little bit carried away in his speech about "fighting vampires on the beaches and in the streets of Scarcombe".

"Yes, sir, only the one – as far as we can ascertain as yet," replied the sergeant as he poked at his carton of raspberry yoghourt with a tea-spoon. "Constables Woolley and Barncastle tracked him down – smart work on their parts. I wonder what gave them the idea of looking in the Ghost Train? They deserve to be a couple of plain-clothes detective constables, don't you think?"

The mayor did not reply. He had not heard what the sergeant had said. His mind was on other things. He was watching, hungrily, as Downend spooned the raspberry yoghourt into his mouth.

Cyril Lightowler had hardly eaten anything at all that evening. Dora had changed her mind about cooking him his toad-in-the-hole. After reading the full report of her husband's town hall speech in the *Evening Chronicle*, Dora had decided that the mayor's place was not at home feeding his face, but at the forefront of the battle. Toad-in-the-hole could wait for less turbulent times: her husband must take himself off with all speed, and spend the night assisting and encouraging the gallant members of the Scarcombe Police Force.

So instead of dining on the promised toad-in-the-hole, Cyril Lightowler had to make do with a hastily assembled tuna-and-cucumber sandwich in wholemeal bread. It had not been anywhere near enough to assuage the hunger pangs of a man who had stood up in front of a packed council chamber and delivered one of the finest speeches ever heard in that ancient hall.

Cyril Lightowler ran his tongue round the inside of his mouth enviously as he watched Sergeant Downend scrape the final spoonful of raspberry yoghourt out of the carton and swallow it down in one gulp.

"Onwards and upwards then, Mr Mayor," said the station sergeant, tossing the empty yoghourt carton into the wastepaper basket. "We'd better get ourselves down to the amusement park in time for the final coup. I'll tell you what, though, just to be on the safe side I'll summon up some assistance first. I'll ring the police station at Seacaster and ask Sergeant Helliwell if he can give us a bit of back-up."

"Are you going to need back-up, Sergeant?" asked the mayor, anxious to get on with things. "If it is just the one vampire?"

Sergeant Downend shrugged. "You never know with vampires, do you, sir?" he asked. "Besides, they've got police dogs at Seacaster. They could prove useful. Would *you* fancy going inside a Ghost Train in the dark, looking for Count Dracula, without a bit of back-up?"

It was a tricky question and one that the mayor decided to pretend he hadn't heard. Meanwhile, the sergeant had picked up the phone and dialled a number. A voice replied at the other end of the line.

"Hello, Alan!" said Sergeant Downend. "It's Brian Downend, Scarcombe, this end. I know it's a funny time of night to ask – but I was wondering if you might give us a bit of back-up and lend us some of your dogs? . . . Yes, of course I'll hang on, chum." Downend put his hand over the telephone's mouthpiece and turned to Lightowler. "He's gone to make enquiries," he whispered.

"I don't suppose, while we're waiting for the back-up team to get over here," began the mayor, tentatively, "that there'll be time for us to pop into the Mermaid Fish and Chip Café for a bite to eat? I'm absolutely famished."

"I shouldn't think so," said Sergeant Downend, with a slow shake of his head. "We'll need to get down to the amusement park as soon as I've made this call. Barncastle and Woolley must need all the help they can get." Downend paused, and his brow wrinkled into a puzzled frown as he continued: "Anyway, doesn't the Mermaid Café belong to Councillor Corcoran? I thought you and he were at daggers drawn? I wouldn't have expected you'd want to be seen dead in his fish-and-chip shop?"

Cyril Lightowler gave a little embarrassed shrug. That was another question that he didn't care to answer. If the truth were to be known, he put the needs of his stomach before any personal quarrels – but he had no intention of letting Sergeant Downend in on that fact.

"I-Spy, With My Little Eye," said Constable Barncastle, "something beginning with F."

"That's easy," replied Woolley, leaning back in the Ghost Train coach and pointing at the decoration on the double doors at the entrance to the ride. "Frankenstein's monster."

"Wrong."

"Go on then – tell me."

"Have another try first."

"No, I give up," said Constable Woolley, who did not feel like playing when there was a blood-drinking vampire in the vicinity. "Tell me."

PC Barncastle smiled craftily, extended an arm

and made a broad sweep all round the amusement park with an extended finger. "F for funfair," he said.

"That isn't fair – it's cheating," objected Woolley. "It isn't called a funfair. It should have been A for amusement park."

"Same difference."

"It isn't the same thing at all," said Woolley, heatedly. "A funfair travels up and down the countryside – an amusement park stops where it is—"

"Hoy!" said a voice in their ears, making them jump and bringing their argument to an end. "What are you two playing at?" The two policemen turned as one, and found themselves looking up into the enquiring face of Reggie Perks. "When the coach stops, the ride's over – you're supposed to get out and walk away," he explained. "Anyway, it's going-home time."

"We're not going anywhere, matey," said Constable Woolley in his best policeman-like manner, rising to his feet. "We're on duty."

"We've got Count Dracula pinned down inside your Ghost Train," explained Barncastle.

"Count Dracula?" The attendant sounded puzzled.

"It's him all right," said Barncastle. "Long black cloak, pointy teeth, bloodshot starey eyes – the lot."

"That's not Count Dracula!" chuckled Mr Perks, unable to hide his amusement. "That's just a chap dressed up pretending to be him. It's usually a mechanical one but that's had to go back to the workshops."

"It's not a chap dressed up at all," said Woolley. "It's the genuine article. He's been terrorising the town for days. Don't say you haven't heard about it?"

"No, I haven't," said the attendant.

"Haven't you read your newspaper?" asked Barncastle, nodding at the *Evening Chronicle* under Mr Perks's arm.

"Only the sports pages."

"Don't you listen to the radio?" asked Woolley.

"Only the football results."

The two policemen both raised their eyebrows as they exchanged a glance.

"Then might I suggest, sir," said Constable Woolley, using his official policeman's voice again, "that you do yourself a favour and examine the front page headlines right this minute?"

"Go on, do it," urged Barncastle as the attendant hesitated. "Do as he says."

Reggie Perks took the newspaper from underneath his arm, unfolded it and, for the first time in his life, looked at the front page.

TOWN TERRORISED BY DARK EVIL FORCES!

it said in enormous black letters across the top and, underneath, in letters that were only slightly smaller, was printed:

FEARLESS MAYOR PLEDGES

"NO SURRENDER"!

"Well, I'm blowed!" said Reggie Perks, his eyes almost popping out of his head. "Aren't you going to go in and arrest him?"

"We're waiting for our back-up team to arrive," explained Woolley.

"I see," said Mr Perks. He folded up his newspaper again, replaced it under one arm and then glanced nervously towards the painting of Frankenstein's monster across the double doors at the entrance to the ride. "Anyway, I won't hang about if you don't mind," he continued briskly. "I have to feed the cat when I get home tonight and she'll be wondering where I've got to. Goodnight, constables." With this he turned quickly and strode off down the Ghost Train's wooden ramp.

Barncastle and Woolley watched as the ride's attendant strode off hastily through the now dark and deserted stalls and sideshows. There was no one left in the entire amusement park except themselves . . . and, of course, the creature inside the Ghost Train.

Norman Woolley shivered, pulled up his jacket collar round his ears and glanced over at the scary picture of Frankenstein's monster just as the attendant had done moments before. "Do you think he was right – should we go in there and see if we can arrest the vampire?"

"It's very dark in there," replied Barncastle, non-committally.

"We've got our torches."

"That's just it . . ." Barncastle hesitated. He had been wanting to get it off his chest all day. Now seemed as good a time as any. ". . . I haven't got my torch. I've lost it."

"Your policeman's torch?" gasped Woolley. "The one you were issued with?"

"Yes. I dropped it last night. In the Chinese pagoda in the ornamental gardens. I thought I saw this vampire bat flitting about up in the rafters. I dropped my torch and ran away. I was too scared to go back and look for it."

Constable Woolley let out a long low whistle under his breath. "Haven't you told *anyone*?" he said.

"Only you."

"You won't half cop it when Sergeant Downend finds out."

"I know . . ." Barncastle hesitated a second time. There was another item of bad news he needed to impart to his colleague, but he wasn't quite sure how best to broach the subject. ". . . Sergeant Downend won't be best pleased with you either, when he finds out."

"Finds out what?"

"That you've lost your helmet."

Constable Woolley's hands flew up to his head and his mouth dropped open in horror. It was true. His helmet wasn't up there in its usual place, sitting on his head.

"You must have lost it in the Ghost Train," Barncastle continued. "I noticed it wasn't there when we came out, but I didn't like to tell you. It must have fallen off when we went round one of those sharp bends."

"That settles it," said Constable Woolley firmly. "I *am* going to go back in there."

"Are you really?"

"And I'm not coming out until I've found that helmet. I'd rather confront a blood-drinking monster than come face to face with Sergeant Downend without it. Are you coming with me, or stopping out here on your own?"

Barry Barncastle glanced round the empty amusement park which suddenly darkened spookily as the moon disappeared behind a low bank of clouds.

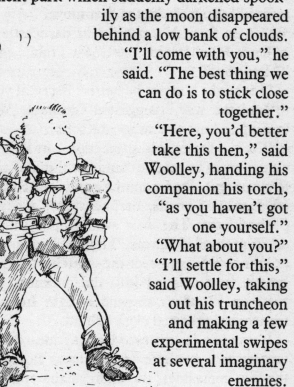

"I'll come with you," he said. "The best thing we can do is to stick close together."

"Here, you'd better take this then," said Woolley, handing his companion his torch, "as you haven't got one yourself."

"What about you?"

"I'll settle for this," said Woolley, taking out his truncheon and making a few experimental swipes at several imaginary enemies.

The two policemen set off along the wooden ramp, past the line of stationary coaches, towards the red-painted double doors beyond which lay total darkness. They came to a halt in front of the painted picture of Frankenstein's monster. Each of the two constables waited for the other one to go first.

Barry Barncastle gazed down at the polished toecaps of his policeman's boots and whistled softly under his breath. Norman Woolley glanced casually above his head and jingled the loose change in his trouser pocket. Neither of them seemed keen to make the first move.

"Go on then, Norman," said Barncastle at last, as he nodded towards the Ghost Train's entrance. "After you."

"I thought it might be better, Barry, if you were to lead the way," suggested Constable Woolley, "seeing as how you've got the torch."

It was a reasonable suggestion and Barry Barncastle, try as he might, could not think of anything to dispute it. Summoning up his courage, he put his free hand on the Frankenstein's monster and pushed hard. The door swung open soundlessly on its well-oiled hinges. The policeman switched on the torch, pressed the switch, took a deep breath, and stepped into the darkness beyond. Norman Woolley, keeping a tight hold on his truncheon, followed close behind.

It was just the moment Count Alucard had been waiting for. As the entrance doors closed behind the two constables, the doors at the opposite end of the Ghost Train's ramp were pushed open from inside. The vampire Count stepped out into the night. He was a little late for his appointment with Henry Hollins, but if he hurried he might still get to the meeting place before the boy gave up waiting for him.

His black cloak billowing out behind him, Count Alucard set off across the concrete concourse of the deserted amusement park and was quickly swallowed up by the night.

8

Henry Hollins realised that all was not going as planned when he heard the incessant barking of a number of dogs on the promenade below.

That same continual sound of yelping dogs exacerbated the nervousness of the wolf pack. Some of them loping singly, others in twos and threes, the wolves bounded restlessly in and out of the pine trees and through the long grass beyond the woods, pausing occasionally to lift their heads and yowl and howl in answer to the distant baying of the dogs. Only Boris stood silent and apart, completely still except for his head which darted from side to side, tongue lolling, as he watched the antics of the pack.

The wily old wolf was fully aware of the pack's growing anxieties – indeed, he himself shared those uncertainties. But he made no attempt to quieten their fears. What would have been the use? The constant barking of the dogs strengthened his belief that something significant was going to happen that night. Something strange. Something unique. Something very important. Something that would change his life and indeed the lives of the entire pack too. The pack's nervousness made Henry Hollins feel on edge outside the compound.

Where was Count Alucard? Had something happened to him? According to the hands on Henry's watch, the vegetarian vampire Count was overdue by a quarter of an hour. Fifteen minutes, Henry argued with himself, was hardly worth worrying about – but another voice told him that Count Alucard was a fussy person who would not be late for an appointment without good reason. And *why* were all those dogs barking in the town below? They must have something to do with the Count's failure to appear.

Perhaps he should set off now and go down into Scarcombe to look for the Count? But that other, wiser voice argued that the best thing he could do would be to stay exactly where he was, and go on waiting . . . and go on hoping . . .

"Quiet, Charles! Down, Edward! Shut up, Andrew! Put a sock in it, Duke! Pack that row in, Queenie! If you don't belt up, Fergie, there'll be trouble!"

But the half-dozen police dogs in the back of the police van continued to yelp and bark and howl, paying not the slightest attention to the commands of the dog handler, Police Constable Russell Purley, sitting in the passenger seat.

"Can I ask you something?" shouted the police driver, to make himself heard above the incessant din coming from the dogs.

"What is it?" Russell Purley shouted back.

"Why did you call them all after the Royal Family?" yelled the driver.

"*I* didn't!" Purley bellowed in return. He nodded at a second police van which was parked on the promenade several yards ahead and inside which were sitting five more constable dog handlers. "You'd better ask them!" he shouted. "Anyway, they're not *all* named after the Royal Family! Only five of them! My one isn't!" As he spoke, the young policeman glanced fondly through the metal grille at the youngest of the six Alsatians.

"What's your one called?" shouted the driver.

"*Beg pardon?*"

"*I said, what's your one called!*"

Constable Purley shouted something in reply which the driver failed to comprehend over the clamour.

118

"*WHAT DID YOU SAY?*" screamed the driver.

"*ELVIS!*"

At which point, all attempts at conversation ended as the two policemen surrendered their losing battle of trying to make themselves heard over the ever-increasing racket coming from the dogs.

The dogs themselves were not entirely to be blamed for kicking up such a fuss. They felt they had been rather badly done by. Dragged from their comfortable kennels, not long after having bedded down for the night, they had been bundled into the back of the police van, driven off along the coast road, and now found themselves parked on the Scarcombe promenade without having any idea of what was going on.

To make things worse, there was a tantalising smell drifting into the police van which tormented the dogs' nostrils, tickled their taste buds and told their stomachs that several hours had elapsed since they had bulged with food.

That selfsame smell, which came from the Mermaid Fish and Chip Café, was the reason why the trio of police vehicles was pulling up along the promenade.

Inside the first van, Police Sergeant Downend glanced impatiently at the light that filtered out on to the pavement from the café.

"Just how long is he going to be?" growled Downend, turning to the driver.

"Search me, Sarge," replied the driver, whose

name was Ashley Seagrove. He sported a slim dark moustache which, at that precise moment, he was trimming with a pair of nail scissors in his rear-view mirror. "I only hope he's not going to leave my vehicle ponging of fish and chips – I've got to pick up the super from the railway station first thing tomorrow morning."

"You shouldn't have pulled up, you know," said Downend angrily. "Just because *he* told you to."

"He is the mayor."

"Mayor he may be – but I'm in charge of this operation, Seagrove. This is an official police convoy and it's been got together to go out after Count Dracula – not to satisfy Cyril Lightowler's craving for fish and chips!" Downend glanced at the last vehicle in the line.

"Can't somebody keep those animals quiet?" he muttered grumpily.

The urgent barking of the police dogs could also be heard inside the Mermaid Fish and Chip Café where the solitary customer, Cyril Lightowler, glowered with growing impatience as the man in the grubby white overall slowly stirred the bubbling contents of the chip pan with a long metal spoon.

"Come on, Councillor!" snapped the mayor at last. "You're holding up an entire police operation, if you did but know it! Can't you speed things up a bit?"

"Sorry, Mr Mayor, but no can do," said Councillor Corcoran and, standing with his back to

Lightowler, he grinned to himself as he gave the chips another lethargic stir. Still smarting over the mayor's jibes at the meeting in the town hall, Colin Corcoran had decided to get a bit of his own back by making the mayor wait for his fish and chips. "It might be possible to rush an item on the agenda through in the council chamber," he continued, "but a chip pan is a law unto itself."

And Councillor Corcoran allowed himself another secretive smile as he watched the sizzling chips turning from a mouth-watering crispy golden colour to an unappetisingly burnt blackened brown.

"Don't play about with it, Barry," said Constable Woolley sharply to his fellow policeman. "You'll only waste the batteries."

"Sorry, Norman," said Constable Barncastle, who had been pointing the torch into the sky and making sweeping searchlight motions with it. "This one's got a terrific beam though, hasn't it? It's brilliant! Much better than the one I lost."

Constable Woolley nodded glumly as they strode out of the deserted moonlit amusement park and on to the promenade. Things were not going quite as well as they might. On the plus side, of course, he had managed to recover his helmet. But on the minus side there had been no sign of the vampire inside the Ghost Train.

Shortly after going through the double doors, the policemen had managed to locate a master

121

switch to illuminate the entire ride. With these lights on, the interior of the Ghost Train was not half as spacious as it had seemed when they had ridden round in the dark. The inside of the ride had appeared large in the dark because the track twisted and turned and doubled back on itself so many times.

The constables realised to their relief that the Ghost Train's many monsters were nowhere near as spooky with the lights switched on as they had appeared to be in the dark either – they were now quite plainly painted creatures fashioned out of wood and wire and *papier maché*.

But, against these pleasant discoveries, the policemen's hearts sank to their boots when the penny dropped that the real life vampire was no longer on the premises. The graveyard tableau was as still and silent as . . . well, as a graveyard. The plywood coffin stood empty. Its occupant had gone. Neither was there any sign of it anywhere inside the ride. Count Dracula had given them the slip. The back-up team would not now be needed. Sergeant Downend would be absolutely furious.

Disconsolately they switched off the lights and went out on to the Ghost Train's ramp. All they could do was to go and confess to Sergeant Downend that they had dragged him out of the warmth and comfort of the police station on a wild goose chase.

Downcast and silent, they walked along the promenade towards the lights of the police vehicles parked outside the Mermaid Fish and Chip

Café. Barncastle absent-mindedly switched on his partner's torch again and, as before, swung the beam in a broad arc across the night sky.

"*Barry!*" snapped Constable Woolley. "How many times do you have to be told? You're not only wasting the batteries now but if Sergeant Downend sees you doing that he's going to go spare! Aren't we in enough hot water as it is, without you making the situation worse?"

"Sorry, Norman, but I just can't get over how brill your torch is," said Barncastle. "Watch this – I can make it shine right across to the cliffs." As he spoke, the constable made a last, lingering sweep with the torch's beam along the cliff face.

Suddenly, and purely by accident, the beam of light picked out a figure halfway up the cliff face, clinging on tightly, inching its way towards the top. Even at that distance, the beam was strong enough for the constables to be able to see that the figure was that of a tall, slim, dark-haired man wearing a black suit, a white shirt, a black bow tie and a long, black, scarlet-lined cloak.

"It's him again, Barry!" cried Woolley, excitedly. "It's Dracula! Don't lose him!"

"I've got him, Norman!" Barncastle replied, taking a tight grip on the torch with both of his hands to steady the beam of light.

"Don't let him get away, Barry!" urged Woolley. "Keep him lit up while I nip down and fetch Sarge and the lads."

As Constable Woolley clattered off along the promenade, Constable Barncastle held the torch steady, its thin shaft of light held tight on the black-cloaked figure scrabbling up the cliff.

When the first beam of light struck him in the face, Count Alucard had remained quite still as though frozen on the side of the cliff. He hoped that whoever was flashing the torch had failed to notice him. But, as the light hovered on and around him, he realised that his presence had been discovered. Shortly afterwards, when he heard the sound of heavy feet along the promenade, accompanied by an increase in the barking of the dogs, the Count knew that it would not be long before all the men below set out in pursuit of him.

The vegetarian vampire Count glanced upwards towards the top of the cliffs which were still a long way off. Although the cliff face was nowhere near perpendicular, it was nevertheless a stiffish, awkward climb – particularly so for someone who had not eaten at all that day, apart from that single, solitary peach.

Count Alucard gulped in the fresh sea air as his breathing returned to normal. Down below, on the promenade, he could hear more running footsteps accompanied by shouted orders and, all the while, the sound of the dogs was growing louder.

"Constables Staveley, Goss and Purley . . ." the voice drifted up the cliff face from below. "*Purley*! Yes, lad, I do mean you! Stop feeding that dog biscuits and pay attention! You three take your dogs and proceed with all speed up the cliffs! The rest of you, follow me! We'll take the vehicles up the cliff road and cut him off at the top!"

The vampire Count was climbing as quickly as he could, but it was a slow and difficult task. His long, thin, delicate fingers struggled to find hand-holds as they probed at the cliff face overhead. His shiny, hand-made, patent leather shoes, which had never been intended for rock-climbing, slipped and slithered and delayed his progress.

Down below he could hear the sound of engines starting up, accompanied by the urgent shouts of the handlers urging on their dogs:

"Get him, Fergie! Go, lass, go!"

"Fetch, Queenie! Fetch, girl, fetch!"

"Come on Elvis, ups-a-daisy! Who's a good police dog then?"

The Count struggled all the harder to scale the cliff face, but the police dog handlers were younger and fitter and were eager for the chase. And they were slowly catching up on him.

"Spread out, lads!" This time the voice came from over his head.

The rest of the police party must have completed the journey up the cliff road in their vehicles and were already preparing to apprehend him at the top. Moments later, another stronger shaft of light from up above his head nearly blinded him.

Count Alucard was trapped. Both from above and from below. Not only that, but the policemen knew that they had their quarry cornered.

"There he is! We've got him now, lads!" A

voice cried out excitedly. A white circle of blinding light encircled the Count. And, all the while, the barking of the dogs below told him that they and their police handlers were drawing ever closer.

But Count Alucard held one ace up his sleeve which his pursuers had not taken into account. Shuffling around, so that his back was pressed against the face of the cliff and his pointed shiny shoes were facing outwards, he took a tight hold on the edges of his black cloak with both of his hands, spread them wide, took a deep breath and launched himself off the precariously narrow ledge of rock out on to the gentle breezes that were coming in from the sea.

Gasps of disbelief and wonder went up from the policemen on the cliff top and the three men struggling with their dogs up the cliff face.

There was absolute silence. Even the police dogs stopped barking or even panting and gazed, slack-jawed and unblinking, at the dark-suited figure hovering on nothingness.

Count Alucard seemed about to plunge onto the rocks below, but, to the astonishment of the watchers both above and beneath, the strangest thing happened. Before their very eyes, the figure began to shrivel and shrink. The black formal suit and shiny patent leather shoes appeared to evaporate in mid-air and in their place fluttered a small, furry-bodied, blunt-nosed, black-eyed creature that now hovered, without fear of falling, on long, slender, dark, parchment-like wings.

Count Alucard, in his fruit bat form, let out a high-pitched joyful shriek as he swooped skywards over the cliff top and then skimmed over the heads of the amazed policemen ranged along the edge.

"Well, I'm blessed!" said Sergeant Downend as the sharp-toothed winged creature swept over his head and then, banking low, flew off in the direction of the Caravan Leisure Park beyond which lay the town's Wildlife Zoo.

"Don't stand there staring, Sergeant!" snapped Cyril Lightowler, who was eating fish and chips in the front seat of the police car parked on the cliff top. "Get after him before he disappears from sight!"

"But he changed into a bat, Mr Mayor, right in front of our eyes!" marvelled the station sergeant.

"Of course he did. What's so unusual about/ that? He's Count Dracula, isn't he? What did you imagine he would change into? A budgerigar? Now, do as I say, and let's get after him before it's too late!"

But the long-winged creature was almost lost to view as it headed inland, shooting over fence and thicket, flying low to shake off any possible pursuers.

"Hello, Henry!" said the voice softly into the boy's ear.

"Wh-wh-wh-what?" stammered Henry Hollins, waking instantly with a start. He'd been waiting so long for his friend that he had fallen asleep leaning against the back wall of the swimming-pool changing rooms.

"I'm sorry," said the Count, changing back into his human form. "I didn't mean to startle you."

"What time is it?"

Count Alucard lifted a slim gold watch by its chain out of his waistcoat pocket. He flipped open the delicate filigreed watch-cover with his thumb-nail and tilted the face towards the moon.

"It's almost half past ten," said the Count. "I do apologise, Henry. Please forgive me. I experienced some slight difficulty in getting away."

"That's all right, Count," said Henry Hollins. "But I'm afraid I won't be able to stay long. Mum and Dad will be going back to the caravan any minute – they're sure to check to see if I'm okay."

As he spoke, Henry Hollins peered round a corner of the changing rooms and looked across the swimming pool to the leisure park's recreational hall. Music was coming from inside the hall with the sound of many voices raised in song. The audience of happy caravaners were singing along with a Talent Contest pop group in the chorus of a Beatles' Sixties pop song. Henry smiled with relief at discovering that the Contest was still going on. And then a puzzling thought occurred to him and his smile faded into a frown.

"That's funny!" said Henry Hollins.

"Something is frightfully amusing?" asked the Count, raising his dark eyebrows questioningly.

"I don't mean that kind of funny," replied Henry with a shake of his head. "It's just that I couldn't hear anything coming from the recreational hall a few minutes ago. The wolves were making too much noise. Now they've stopped completely." He paused and nodded at the wire-mesh fence. "It's all gone quiet in there now."

It was true. There was not so much as a whimper now from the compound where a short time ago the wolf pack had been howling without pause.

It was the turn of the vampire Count to smile. "They are my children of the night," he said, wrapping his cloak round himself. "They know that they have nothing to fear when I am near."

"The wolves are your friends?" asked Henry

129

Hollins in some surprise.

"Of course. Why not? We have much in common, those wolves and I. The tranquil silence of the snow-filled winters; the awesome peace of the wide-ranging forests. Some of them remember the old days, some do not – but all of them have Transylvania in their blood, as I have myself." There was a faraway look in Count Alucard's eyes. "One day, Henry Hollins, those wolves and I will share—"

But Henry Hollins was not going to find out exactly what it was that the Scarcombe Wildlife Zoo wolf pack and the Transylvanian vampire Count were one day going to share. For the Count's words had been interrupted by the sound of the police dogs barking not far off, an indication that the dogs, accompanied by their handlers, were approaching fast.

"What's all that about?" asked Henry, puzzled. "I heard those dogs earlier down on the promenade, but I couldn't see from here what was going on. It was that same barking that set off the wolf pack's howling."

"That, Henry, is the slight difficulty that I mentioned earlier. I'm afraid that they are police dogs and it is I whom they are looking for. I thought I had managed to shake them off – alas, it seems I was not that fortunate."

"They're sending *dogs* to track you down?" asked Henry, outraged.

"So it would appear," sighed the Count.

"*Dogs!*" repeated Henry angrily. "How can they

130

do that? You wouldn't harm a fly. You haven't *done* anything!"

"It is my unfortunate lot in life to have been born a Dracula," said the Count, giving a hopeless little shrug of his shoulders. "Around the world wherever I go my name alone is sufficient to condemn me." He paused. The yelping of the approaching dogs was growing louder by the second. "Do me a favour, Henry Hollins, would you?" asked the vampire Count. "Peep round that corner and tell me what you see – if I show myself they may get scent of me."

Henry peered, then quickly turned back and gulped.

"They're on the other side of the swimming pool already," said the boy. "There's lots of them: policemen and dogs. They've got torches too, and more are coming through the caravan park. They'll be here in a minute. You've got to get away, Count Alucard. You *must*! Change into a bat and fly away before it's too late."

"And leave you here to face them on your own?" Count Alucard shook his head, slowly but firmly. "They will question you. A boy? Out here alone? What would you tell them?"

"The truth," said Henry solemnly. "That you are my friend. That you are kind and good and gentle and that you wouldn't—"

"No, no, no," the Count interrupted. "That would not do at all, Henry Hollins. A boy admitting to consorting with a Transylvanian vampire Count? My goodness me – even admitting you had

131

met me would bring their wrath down upon your head."

"But what *are* you going to do then, Count?" demanded Henry.

"Do you trust me, Henry?" asked the Count.

"Of course I do! You know I do."

"Then take my hand," said the Count.

Henry did as he had been asked and allowed himself to be led off along the the side of the wire-mesh fence. The Count moved with smooth, easy strides on his long legs and the boy had difficulty in keeping up with his friend. But they had not far to travel before they arrived at a disused gate almost obscured by weeds, which opened into the compound.

"Here is one place where they will not dare to follow," said the Count, "but the only problem, Henry, is whether you will dare to come with me?"

"I said I trusted you, Count," said the boy who, after quickly swallowing hard, did not take more than a moment to make up his mind. "But how can you get in? It's locked." As he spoke, Henry pointed at the rusted chain which was held in place by an equally rusted padlock.

"There are occasional moments, even in my hectic life, when being a Dracula does have its advantages," said the Count with a wry smile. "There are some talents which I have inherited from my forebears."

Count Alucard took a bunch of curious, flat keys out of a pocket in the scarlet lining of his voluminous cloak. Quickly selecting one of the keys, he slipped it into the keyhole, gave a couple of adept twists and the padlock cranked open. He pushed at the gate which opened slowly, forcing its way through the accumulation of weeds. They stepped inside and the Count turned and shut the gate tightly behind them.

"Well, Henry Hollins?" said the Count, looking into the dark, thickly wooded area where the wolf pack was gathered. "Shall we take our chances?"

But Henry Hollins did not hesitate. Again giving Count Alucard his hand, the boy allowed his friend to lead him into the trees and into the company of the wolves.

9

"Search boy, search! Go get 'im, Andy!"

"Go on, Queenie! Let's get that vampire, eh?"

"Here, Eddie! Roust him out, boy!"

"Fetch, Fergie! Fetch, lass!"

"Go, Charles, go! Let's show 'em, lad!"

With shouts of encouragement, the occasional reproving command and a piercing whistle, the dog handlers stumbled about in the long grass beyond the Caravan Leisure Park's swimming pool, bumping into fellow constables as they searched for their quarry. The moon disappeared behind a convenient cloud and the forces of law and order fell into disarray.

The dogs managed to pick up Count Alucard's scent in the spot behind the changing rooms. Unfortunately, though, they lost the trail a short time later. They picked up instead the scent of a hedgehog which had passed that way some hours before and which, as far as the police dogs were concerned, had left a far more interesting pong than that of the vampire Count.

"Elvis! *Elvis*! *Bad* dog! Stop that!" shouted Constable Russell Purley.

Elvis, having sniffed out the lingering whiff of

134

fish and chips on the town's mayor, was leaping up clumsily at that civic dignitary and endeavouring to lick his face.

"Get down! Get it down! Get it off me!" snarled Cyril Lightowler, pushing at the police dog with both hands and wishing that he had had the sense to stay in the police car.

Splash!

"Please can somebody bring a torch over here!" cried the voice of Constable Barry Barncastle, who had used up the batteries in his borrowed torch long before. "Constable Woolley's fallen into the swimming pool!"

"Oh, no!" grumbled Sergeant Downend to himself as he strove to reorganise the search which was beginning to get out of hand. "What's going to happen to us next?"

What happened next made matters even worse.

As the dog handlers and their fellow policemen struggled to pick up the vampire's trail again, they were hampered in their attempts as the exit doors of the recreational hall were pushed open and the audience at the end of the evening's Talent Contest burst outside.

In the forefront of this crowd of carefree caravaners was the elderly lady in the grass skirt and the bikini top who was triumphantly holding aloft the large bottle of bubble-bath which she had won.

"What's this?" moaned Sergeant Downend, as the crowd of holiday-makers surged inquisitively towards the area where the search was taking place. "Get back! Get back, all of you!" yelled Downend. "This is a security operation! It's a no-go area for anybody who isn't a policeman!"

But the station sergeant's demands for the crowd to disperse seemed to have entirely the opposite effect. The more Downend begged, entreated and threatened, the more the crowd pushed forward, intent on enjoying this free entertainment.

"Will you all go to your caravans, *please*!" pleaded the police sergeant. "I beg of you, for your own sakes! We have reason to suspect that Count Dracula is somewhere in the vicinity!"

But even this last awesome disclosure did nothing to deter the gaping throng. Not a bit of it. Quite the reverse, in fact. After all, the faint-hearted among the holiday-makers had packed their bags and driven out of the camp that morning – many of those who had stayed behind had done so in the hope of catching a glimpse of the infamous blood-drinking Count. The revelation that he was actually somewhere close to the leisure park excited them to fever pitch. Instead of retiring, they pressed forward all the more in order to gain a better view.

In spite of all Sergeant Downend's efforts in enlisting several of his constables to hold back the crowd, the holiday-makers had pushed the policemen out of the way and were trampling down the grassy areas, hindering the police dogs and their handlers, and generally getting in the way of the police, as they tried to look for clues which might lead to the vampire's whereabouts.

"Ouch!" said Sergeant Downend, as someone trod on his foot. He turned to find himself confronting a man with a red false nose, a lampshade on his head and, under one arm, a ghastly coloured, hideous teddy bear.

"Sorry!" said the man who had been awarded the First Prize in the Talent Contest.

Before Sergeant Downend could question this curiously garbed chap, a voice called out to him from over by the wire fence.

"Sergeant Downend! Come and take a look at this!"

The station sergeant pushed his way through the holiday-makers, past the swimming pool where the luckless Constable Woolley, having recently fallen in, was sitting sodden on a plastic chair emptying the water out of his boots, across to where Constable Purley and his police dog, Elvis, were standing by the gate half hidden by tall weeds.

"What do you make of this, Sarge?" asked the constable, holding out the padlock and the rusty chain. "Somebody's gone through this gate not long ago."

"Well done, lad," said Downend, taking the chain and padlock out of Purley's hands and giving them a cursory inspection.

"It wasn't me that found them – it was Elvis," lied Russell Purley, hoping to get his dog back into the sergeant's good books again after its bad behaviour with the mayor.

"Woof-woof!" barked Elvis loudly, wagging his tail and looking up eagerly into the station sergeant's face.

Sergeant Downend nodded disinterestedly, then peered through the wire-mesh fence and over into the dark woods. He really didn't care a brass farthing whether it had been the dog or the policeman who had found the padlock and the chain. Neither did he blame the dog for trying to lick the mayor's face. It was the mayor's own stupid fault anyway. Cyril Lightowler hadn't any business to be here – hanging about, trying to steal the glory. But if Count Dracula *had* gone through the gate and was lying in hiding in those woods, would Cyril Lightowler dare to go in there, regardless of the wolf pack, and arrest the evil blood-drinking monster? Of course he wouldn't! Never in a million years! No, tasks like that could only be carried out by a man of courage. A valorous man who knew not fear and strode where others did not dare to tread . . .

"Do you think he is inside those woods, Sarge?" Purley's voice broke in on the station sergeant's thoughts. "Should we go in there and look for him?"

"Are you crackers, lad?" sneered Downend, coming back to earth from his heroic fantasy. "There's an entire wolf pack in those woods. Anybody who goes in there would need his brains washing!"

"So what do we do then, Sergeant?" asked the puzzled policeman. "If Dracula's in there and we're out here – how do we set about catching him?"

"We wait, Constable," replied the police sergeant ponderously. "Softlee, softlee, catchee monkee. We wait out here all night, if necessary."

"Right, Sarge," replied Purley.

"He's got to come out some time," continued Downend, "and when he does, we'll be here to nab him."

Police Constable Purley nodded and tried to look enthusiastic. Although it had occurred to him that the vampire could change himself into a bat again and easily make his escape long before morning, he had no wish to argue with the station sergeant.

"I wish we could get shot of this lot though," growled Downend, indicating the throng of holiday-makers. "It would serve them right if Dracula were to nip out of those woods this instant and bite a few of them on their necks! You'd think that some of them, at least, would have the commonsense to get themselves indoors."

To give the caravaners their due, several did have the commonsense to go off to the safety of their leisure park homes. Emily and Albert, to name but two, had returned to their mobile home as soon as they had heard about the possible presence of the vampire. They were not concerned about their own welfare but, as loving parents, they were worried about the well-being of their son.

Their worst fears were all too soon confirmed.

"He's not here, Albert!" Emily gasped as she peeped into Henry's bedroom. "Wherever can the boy have got to? Did he say anything to you about going out?"

Albert Hollins dolefully shook his head. There was no way of knowing where he'd gone. It was just as well that Emily and Albert did not know where their son was, for if they had known Henry's whereabouts their concern would have doubled.

Henry Hollins stood quite still in the silvery moonlight at Count Alucard's side, and held his breath as he stared at the wolves surrounding them. Henry, his fingers crossed and his arms straight down by his sides, blinked nervously, gulped twice, and wondered what was going to happen next.

He had watched as one by one the wolves had padded out of the shadows and formed a circle round them. The wolves in fact were just as nervous of Count Alucard and Henry as Henry was of them.

It was the very first time that most of the wolves had been so close to any humans – and particularly without a wire-mesh fence to separate them. But even if their packleader, Boris, had not warned the pack to keep their distance from the visitors, the wolves would still not have felt any animosity towards the boy-cub and the adult male. Not a bit of it.

The wolves had sensed that the larger of the two had some kind of mystical importance. It was because of him, they sensed, that there were more humans out there, beyond the compound, disturbing the night with flashing lights and barking dogs. But the wolves did not answer the dogs' barking, as they had done earlier that night, with yowls and howls and bayings at the moon. Instead, they stood in a ring round these two humans and waited patiently for events to take their turn.

They did not have long to wait.

Boris padded up to Count Alucard. They held each other's gaze for several moments, while Henry Hollins and the wolf pack watched with bated breath. Then, at last, the vampire Count stretched out a long, pale hand for Boris to sniff the slender fingers.

"Hello, Boris, old friend," said Count Alucard, dropping on to one knee and cradling the aged

wolf's scarred head in his hands. "It's been a long, long time since we wandered together in the forest."

Boris, who had not only recognised the voice but understood what the Count said, let out a soft, crooning whine full of pleasure, pity and a craving for affection.

"You know him then?" asked Henry Hollins with surprise.

"I know several of them," replied the Count. "They are from my homeland. I know them from the old days. But this one . . ." as he spoke, Count Alucard gently stroked Boris's head, ". . . this old fellow I know especially well."

Several of the older wolves padded forward and pushed their noses up against the vampire's middle. Then, gaining confidence, a couple of the younger wolves, Igor and Ivan, also joined in, pushing their heads forward to be patted and stroked.

"Patience, children, patience!" cried the Count. "I only possess one pair of hands."

Then Henry Hollins, growing in confidence as he realised there was nothing to fear, put out a hand and patted the flank of one of the younger wolves. The Count smiled and nodded encouragingly.

"Good," said the Count. "Well done, Henry Hollins. It is good that you have taken to each other. We are safe with the children of the night. No harm will come to us."

"I've just remembered something," said Henry, digging his hands into his jacket pockets and pulling out the fruit that he had been carrying around. He proffered the plums to the vegetarian vampire. "I've brought you something else to eat," he said, and then added, ruefully: "I'm afraid one of them's got just a bit squashed."

"Not at all!" replied the Count, his dark eyes flashing with keen anticipation of the joyous taste to come. "Why, they look in excellent condition. This morning you treated me to a peach – tonight you have arranged a feast of plums! Was ever a man so rich in friendship?"

As he spoke, Count Alucard sank his sharp teeth into the deep-purplish skin of one of the plums and bit off a sizeable mouthful which he chewed with relish. Henry watched in silence for several seconds as the Count spat out a plum stone into an open hand and then began to eat a second plum with equal enjoyment without a care in the world.

"But what are you going to *do*, Count?" asked the boy, unable to contain his fears for his friend.

143

"You can't stay in here with the wolves for ever. What's going to happen when morning comes? As soon as it gets light, they're sure to come looking for you."

"Don't worry, Henry," replied the Count, taking his black silk handkerchief out of a pocket and fastidiously wiping the plum juice from his fingers. "I'm sure that with the assistance of our friends here . . ." as he spoke, Count Alucard fondled one of Boris's battle-scarred ears, ". . . we shall be able to walk out of this place whenever it suits us."

"I only wish I knew how!" muttered Henry, puzzled.

The Count lowered his head and whispered something to the leader of the wolf pack. The old wolf growled softly in reply, then turned and padded off towards the thickest part of the woods. He paused by the fringe of tall trees and turned his head to look back at his followers and the man and the boy standing in the circle. One by one, the wolves moved across to form a group behind their leader.

"Come," said the Count to Henry. "It is time for us to go."

Henry Hollins, still no wiser as to what the Count and the wolves intended doing, set off beside his friend. The wolf pack silently padded on ahead across the fine carpet of pine needles into the woods.

"This is stupid!" grumbled Police Constable Norman Woolley as he changed out of his sodden uniform in the back of a police van into a pair of green corduroy trousers, some sneakers, a pair of yellow socks, and a gaily coloured beach shirt with HOLLYWOOD printed in big letters across the back – all of which had been lent to him by a kindly caravaner. "What are we supposed to be doing here anyway?" continued the constable as he gazed out at the crowds of holiday-makers mingling still with the growing mass of policemen, as reserves of village constables summoned in by radio-telephone from outlying districts joined the throng.

"Sergeant Downend thinks he's got Count Dracula surrounded," said Police Constable Barry Barncastle.

"*Surrounded*?" scoffed Woolley, disbelievingly. "How can you surround Count Dracula, Barry? He's a vampire. He can change into a flippin' bat whenever he feels like it. He can *fly*!"

"I know, Norman," said Barncastle, a trifle nervously, remembering again the shadowy, fluttering object that he might – or might not – have spotted the night before in the red-gold rafters of the Chinese pagoda in the oriental gardens.

"Look out, Barry!" yelled Constable Woolley, as a large dark object bounded into the back of the van.

Barry Barncastle let out a little cry of panic and surprise as he felt himself bowled over backwards on to the hard floor of the police van by the big dark object which then pinned him to the floor with its forefeet planted firmly on his chest. The thing lowered its head and with a long, rough tongue slobbered all over his face.

"Get it off me!" wailed Constable Barncastle.

"It's all right, Barry," panted Constable Woolley, tugging at the animal's neck. "It's not a vampire – it's only a dog."

"Sandy? Sandy!" called out Stanley Penworthy, the burger-chef, peering into the back of the van. "Are you in there?"

"Is this your dog?" snapped Constable Woolley, still struggling to pull the cocker spaniel off his friend.

"Yes. Is he being a bother? He's only trying to be friendly."

"That's not the point," said Woolley as the burger-chef succeeded in getting hold of Sandy and dragging him out of the van. "He should be on a lead, you know," continued the policeman. "There's an important police operation going on here. He'll hamper our dogs."

"I'm sorry," said Mr Penworthy. "Actually, he *was* on a lead. But he managed somehow to slip out of his collar." To prove what he was saying, the burger-chef held up a dog's collar and lead, and then continued: "What's happening exactly? Is it that vampire again?"

"I'm afraid we're not at liberty to say," said Norman Woolley stiffly.

"If it *is* Count Dracula, you can tell me," said Mr Penworthy proudly. "I'm Stanley Penworthy.

This is my dog, Sandy. We had our pictures in yesterday's *Evening Chronicle*. We were the ones who found the coffin on the sands. It was us that first disturbed the vampire."

"It might have been best if you'd left well alone," snapped Constable Barncastle who had just managed to sit up again and was wiping the slobber off his face with his uniform sleeve. "It might have been best for everybody," added the policeman, "if you'd minded your own business."

"Be like that," said Stanley Penworthy grumpily. Up until that moment he had seen himself as the hero of Scarcombe – even though he had run away when the vampire Count had sat up in his coffin – and he was put out at suddenly being blamed for everything. "Come on, Sandy!" he said, moving off into the night.

"That's told him, Barry," said Constable Woolley. "You certainly put him in his place."

"You don't think I was a little hard on him, do you, Norman?" asked Constable Barncastle.

"Not at all, Barry," said Woolley stoutly. "You only told the truth."

"Well, yes, I suppose I did," said Barry Barncastle. "If he hadn't disturbed the vampire, our chaps might have nabbed it yesterday morning while it was still in its coffin."

"I wonder," said a voice, "if you would care to make a statement to that effect?"

The two policemen glanced towards the open doors at the back of the van where, framed in the moonlight, stood the raincoated figure of Royston

Renshaw, the reporter from the *Scarcombe Evening Chronicle*.

The newspaperman had been watching that evening's entertainment in the recreational hall with a view to writing an article about it in the next day's paper. But these goings on outside offered him a far better news story than the one about the first prize in the Talent Contest being won by a man with a lampshade on his head who juggled with two oranges and an apple. The only problem so far had been that the reporter had not found anyone with time to tell him what exactly was going on. All the policemen he met were far too busy rushing hither and thither trying to control the crowds to spare him so much as a moment of their time. But suddenly his luck had turned.

Or had it?

"I beg your pardon?" said Constable Barncastle, peering out at the reporter.

"Royston Renshaw, *Scarcombe Evening Chronicle*," said the newspaperman, in his best reporter's voice. "I was just wondering if you'd care to make a statement about what's going on?"

"No comment," said Constable Woolley, using the words which, during his training, he had been taught to use on such occasions as these.

"I was speaking to the constable," said Renshaw coldly.

"I *am* a constable," replied Woolley, equally coldly.

"If you're a constable, why are you wearing corduroy trousers and a shirt with 'HOLLY-

WOOD' written across the back?"

"Push off," said Woolley irritably and he leant across to pull the van's rear doors shut in Royston Renshaw's face.

"That's telling him, Norman," said Barncastle with a wry chuckle, using the words that his companion had used not long before about Stanley Penworthy. "You certainly put him in his place."

"You don't think I was too hard on him, do you, Barry?" asked Constable Woolley, echoing, in his turn, the words that Barncastle had previously used. "Only I wasn't going to let him know that I'd fallen into the swimming pool. I wouldn't want that to get into tomorrow's *Evening Chronicle*."

"No, I don't suppose you would," said Barncastle, giving his colleague a sympathetic smile.

Poor old Norman, thought Constable Barncastle, he really does look down in the dumps. And no wonder. It hadn't been much of a night for him so far. Losing his helmet in the Ghost Train, and then, when he had got it back, falling into the leisure park's swimming pool.

"Tell me again about your Formation Dancing Team?" said Barncastle, in an attempt to take his chum's mind off the evening's disasters. "Which night of the week did you say you practise?"

"Every Wednesday in the Market Hall," said Woolley, brightening immediately at the prospect of discussing his favourite subject. "Why? Do you think you might like to have a bash at it?"

"I might do, Norman," said Barry Barncastle,

nodding thoughtfully. "Yes – one of these fine Wednesday evenings, I might just give it a go . . ." He paused, frowned, pulled a face and then added: "I don't suppose I'd be much good at it, though."

"You never know what you're capable of until you try, do you?" said Constable Woolley. "I bet you'd enjoy it. We wear these sort of black Spanish suits with silver piping down the trousers and short, tight jackets with padded shoulders and mother-of-pearl buttons."

"Really? That sounds exciting," said Constable Barncastle, perking up. "And do you think there might be a place in the team for me?"

"There's one going at this very moment, Barry. Deborah Padbury's looking for a partner. Laurence Peasegood – the chap she used to dance with – is having to knock it on the head. His wife's just joined the Badminton Club and that meets on Wednesday nights as well. She's put her foot down rather heavily as far as Laurence's dance nights are concerned. Wednesday night is babysitting night for him in future."

"What's she like, this Deborah Padbury?"

"Debbie? She's great! She's got a fantastic sense of humour. You ought to hear her laugh! She's a waitress at the Grenadier Grill in Town Street. You want to come next Wednesday, Barry, and get your name down – smartly."

"Do you want to know something, Norman? I might just do that very thing. Tell me some more about this Formation Dancing lark."

"Well, first of all . . ."

Constable Barncastle leant forward showing a keen interest as Constable Woolley explained the ins and outs of the competitive pastime that he loved.

Outside the police van a fearful hullabaloo broke out. There was shouting, there was barking, there was a howling and there was a yowling – there was sufficient noise to wake up the departed souls in Scarcombe's Public Cemetery several miles away. But the two policemen sitting in the back of the van were too caught up in the enthralling world of Formation Dancing to be aware that anything out of the ordinary was taking place.

10

It was curious that the first person to spot the wolf pack's escape was not one of Sergeant Downend's sharp-eyed force but the elderly lady in the grass skirt still carrying her prize jar of bubble-bath. Not that it occurred to her, when she chanced to see Mikhail loping easily across the spare ground, that she was looking at a wolf. Not at all. The elderly lady assumed it was a police dog that had slipped its leash.

But when Mikhail was closely followed by the lean-flanked Igor flashing his grey-green eyes, then by Relka with the fearsome silver blaze right down her back and her fangs gleaming, the elderly lady was forced to think again.

"Wolves! Wolves!" she screamed, clutching the jar of bubble-bath tightly to her bikini top. "The wolves are out!"

"Wolves! Wolves!" The cry was taken up by a score of voices as more members of the wolf pack raced to and fro across the grassy area between the wire-mesh fence and the edge of the Caravan Leisure Park, brushing in, out, around and through the crowd of terrified caravaners.

"What's happening?" called Cyril Lightowler,

winding down the window of the parked police car where he was taking a breather.

"The wolves are loose!" yelled Sergeant Downend frantically, as he bravely raced towards the centre of the hubbub.

"Wolves?" gasped the mayor, hastily winding up the window. Then, after locking the door, he decided to take no further part in the night's proceedings.

After struggling hard to control their charges as the wolves snapped and snarled cheekily at the police dogs' heels, the dog handlers were forced to release their hold on the Alsatians.

For several very long minutes joyful animal pandemonium reigned.

Lenin and Tanya frisked with Charles and Fergie. Ivan and Tracey romped with Andrew and Duke across the spare ground. Lenin, Dushka and Kevin played at catch-as-catch-can with Edward. Elvis sniffed at Olga's rear end and got a sharp reprimanding nip on his own rear end in return. Kevin, the youngest wolf, quite overcome by his first taste of freedom, was more than content to revolve in circles in pursuit of his own tail, watched at a safe distance by Sandy, the cocker spaniel. In short, there were wolves and dogs jumping, bounding, leaping, snarling, snapping, yowling and yapping all over the place.

Every dog shall have his day, or so the saying goes, but on this occasion it was more a case of both dogs and wolves making the most of what was proving to be *their* night. And, while the animals ruled the roost, the policemen ran this way and that, blowing their whistles and flashing their torches, while the caravaners ran that way and this in their attempts to flee from the scene.

It was simplicity itself, while all of this was going on, for Count Alucard, Henry Hollins and Boris to slip out through the compound gate. They turned their backs on the continuing rumpus and walked off towards the peace and quiet of the cliff tops.

"I can't stay long though, Count," said Henry. "Mum and Dad will be wondering where I've got to."

"Please, Henry Hollins, do not cause your parents any anxiety on my account," said Count Alucard, ruffling the thick fur at the back of the wolf's neck. "And Boris, you must be getting back soon to your friends too."

"Shall I see you again tomorrow?" asked Henry, hesitant to leave without making arrangements for their next meeting.

"Why not?" smiled the Count. "We could meet here on the top of the cliffs tomorrow afternoon. Shall we say three o'clock?"

"Will it be safe for you to come?"

"I think so," said Count Alucard, glancing back at the flashing lights and the shouts and barks and wolf howls. "I imagine that the powers-that-be will have problems enough to contend with tomorrow without worrying over-much about me. Goodnight to you, Henry Hollins."

"Goodnight, Count Alucard," said Henry. "I'll

see you tomorrow."

With that, Henry turned and scampered off in the direction of the Caravan Leisure Park. Luckily, when he arrived back, his parents were far too interested in the tumult coming from beyond the swimming pool to scold him for staying out beyond his bedtime.

"You're late, young man," said Albert Hollins, standing framed in the open doorway of their mobile home.

"Sorry, Dad," said Henry.

"We were getting very worried, Henry," said Emily, "especially with all that fuss and bother going on."

"Sorry, Mum," said Henry. "I won't do it again."

As Henry Hollins mounted the steps he gave a last glance towards the cliff tops where, by the light of the moon, he could just make out the silhouette of the cloaked figure standing exactly where he'd left him, gazing out across the bay towards the horizon, with the old wolf still at his side.

"That thing's got to go for a start!" said Police Superintendent Harvey Heathcote, scowling across at the ominous black polished coffin propped up in a corner of his office. "It gives me the heebie-jeebies."

The superintendent had returned that very morning from a holiday in sunny Florida with his wife, Cecily, and their nine-year-old twins, Michael and Michelle.

"Sorry, Super," said Sergeant Downend. "We only put it in here on a temporary basis."

"That's true, Harvey," said Cyril Lightowler, who was sitting opposite the superintendent. He'd walked over to the police station in the hope of clearing up the problems he had helped to create the night before. "We weren't expecting you to come in until tomorrow."

"It's a good job I *have* come in today," growled the superintendent, thumbing through the sheaf of incident reports pertaining to the previous night's happenings piled on his desk, "if this lot's anything to go by!"

"Did you have a nice holiday, Harvey?" asked

the mayor, in an attempt to put the superintendent into a better humour. "How was Disney World? Did you, by any chance, spot Mickey and Minnie Mouse?"

"Never mind Disney World!" snapped the superintendent. "It's what has been happening here in Scarcombe that is more to the point. And what did *you* think you were up to, Sergeant Downend, calling out all those police dogs and summoning reinforcements?"

"It seemed like a good idea at the time, Super," mumbled the sergeant, giving an apologetic little shrug.

"And then there's all this business about the wolves escaping from the Wildlife Zoo. Who do you think is going to come on holiday here if it gets about that the town's riddled with vampires and rotten with wolves?"

"I suppose it did all get a little out of hand, Harvey," said Cyril Lightowler with a sigh. "The keepers managed to recapture all the wolves. They've got them in cages until it's been decided what to do with them."

"They can't stay in Scarcombe, that's for sure," said the superintendent. "We can't take the chance of that happening again. A party of senior citizens is arriving at the railway station this morning. How do you think they're going to feel when they see this afternoon's *Evening Chronicle*? Wolves and vampires indeed! A fine outlook for an old folks' holiday! They'll be high-tailing it out of Scarcombe in droves. Straight off to Bridling-

157

ton, I shouldn't wonder, as fast as their zimmer frames can carry them."

"Do you think it will be in the *Chronicle*?" asked Sergeant Downend dismally.

"It's bound to be," said Cyril Lightowler. "I saw that Royston Renshaw wandering about last night with his notebook and ballpoint in his fist."

"It'll be front page news then," said the super-intendent sorrowfully. "You know what Renshaw's like when he gets his nose into a story. It'll be blown up out of all proportion too, if I know that reporter."

"That's not all, Harvey," said the mayor hesi-tantly. "I understand that someone let it slip to him that one of your constables had the great misfortune to fall into the leisure park's swimming pool."

"Oh, no!" groaned the superintendent, putting his head into his hands. "My police force is going to be the laughing stock of Scarcombe. Which constable was fool enough to do a thing like that?"

"Constable Woolley," said Sergeant Downend.

"I might have guessed as much," said the superintendent.

"He's all right, though," added the sergeant, trying to look on the bright side. "Constable Barncastle pulled him out."

"He would!" snapped Superintendent Heath-cote. "He'd have done better to have left him where he was. They make a good pair, those two. I'm dreading this afternoon's *Chronicle*. If only there was something we could do to stop the editor printing Renshaw's article."

"Perhaps there is . . ." said the mayor thoughtfully. "He wouldn't publish what Renshaw has written if he had a better story for his front page, would he?"

"No, I don't suppose he would," said the superintendent. "But nothing more is likely to happen in Scarcombe, is it?"

"Oh, I don't know," said Cyril Lightowler. "Perhaps we might be able to organise something. I've got a little plan that might serve to kill two birds with one stone. Do you mind if I use your telephone? I need to make several phone calls."

"Be my guest, Cyril," said the puzzled police superintendent.

Cyril Lightowler picked up the telephone from the superintendent's desk and dialled the operator. "What number do I dial," he asked, "if I want to make an overseas call?"

"Overseas?" wailed Heathcote. "That'll cost a bomb!"

"It might be worth it," said the mayor sharply, dialling the number that the operator gave him, "if it gets us out of the mess we're in."

"Och, mon, and what kind o' a cargo do you call yon?" growled Hamish McWhister, watching from the paint-peeled bridge of *La Bernache* as the crane on the harbour lowered another crate into the ship's hold.

Inside the crate, Boris peered out through the

159

bars at the crates containing his followers which were already in the hold.

"I call it a cargo for which we are being well paid to carry across your English Channel, M'sieur McWhister," replied Captain André Amiens curtly. "You should be grateful that we are not sailing back to the Continent with an empty hold."

"It's no' *my* English Channel, mon! I'm a Scot!" grumbled the grumpy ship's mate. "Hoots, mon – if I dinna get masel' transferred to a better boat than this, ma name's no' Hamish McWhister! A hold full o' dangerous animals and a ship's galley wi'out a cook inside it to make so much as a bowlful of porridge!"

"Every cloud has a silver lining, *mon ami*," said the Belgian sea captain, puffing on the stub of his black cigar and peering out across the harbour towards Scarcombe's seafront. "If the cook had not been taken ill with – 'ow-you-say, tummy trouble, we would not have to put into this port. And, if we had not docked here, we wouldn't have secured this valuable commission."

"Valuable commission!" stormed McWhister. "Is that what you call it? Shipping wild beasties across to the Continent! Why, mon—" The ship's mate broke off and then let out another cry of despair as he caught sight of the last item of the ship's cargo which was just being lifted on board. "Oh, no! Not that thing back again! I thought that yon devilish article was sitting at the bottom of Davy Jones's locker the noo!"

McWhister was referring to the black polished

coffin which was being craned towards the open hold.

"Calm yourself, *m'sieur*," purred the captain. "There is nothing to fear on this occasion, and unlike the voyage coming over, this time the box is empty."

"Empty or full, Captain," growled the ship's mate, "there's bad luck attached to that infernal object. It's Dracula's coffin, mon, is yon – and wherever that foul contrivance goes, you can be sure its owner isnae far away."

Then, after watching the coffin disappear into the hold, the ship's mate showed his disgust by striding out of the wheelhouse and slamming the door shut noisily behind him. He set off towards the galley where, in the absence of the ship's cook and to his own further annoyance, Hamish McWhister would have to make his own cup of cocoa.

Alone on the bridge, Captain Amiens smiled to himself as he considered the superstitious nature of his Scottish mate.

But the canny Scottish ship's mate had been close to the truth when he had spoken of the close proximity of the vampire Count. As McWhister uttered those words, Count Alucard and Henry Hollins were sitting on top of the cliff, watching the coffin and the wolves being loaded on to the cargo boat. They had just been looking at the early edition of the *Scarcombe Evening Chronicle*, brought along by Henry for his friend's benefit. It carried a front page story of interest to them both:

WOLVES TO BE RETURNED TO THE WILD

This was printed in big, black, bold letters across the top of the page, while lower down, in slightly smaller letters and above a photograph of Cyril Lightowler in his mayoral official regalia, was a second headline:

SCARCOMBE TWINNED WITH TRANSYLVANIAN TOWN

The story which accompanied these headlines, stemming from an exclusive interview granted to Royston Renshaw by the mayor himself, told of the recent decrease in numbers of the Central European wolf in its natural habitat. In order to halt this sad decline, the mayor of Scarcombe had spoken to his opposite number in Tolokovin, a small town in Upper Transylvania, and had offered to despatch the Scarcombe Wildlife Zoo's own wolf pack, so that it could be let loose in the vast forests surrounding the town.

This kind offer was accepted immediately. What's more, the link between the two communities was to be further extended by the twinning of the towns. There would be a number of benefits for both communities. In the very near future, the Tolokovin town council was to host a visit from the Scarcombe councillors. A banquet in the Tolokovin Town Hall was being arranged. Not only

162

that, but a reciprocal visit by the town councillors of Tolokovin to Scarcombe was already in the pipeline. Joyous and memorable municipal functions would be enjoyed by councillors all.

According to the newspaper story, the twinning of the towns was a wonderful thing. Cyril Lightowler, it said, was a credit to Scarcombe and Scarcombe should be duly proud of its mayor. In writing up his article, Royston Renshaw had decided that it might not be a bad idea if he were to butter up the mayor a little. After all, there would probably be a spare seat going for some lucky journalist on the trip to the banquet in Transylvania. If he played his cards correctly, he could well be that fortunate chap.

"It doesn't say anything at all in the newspaper about what happened last night with the wolves and the dogs and everything?" said a puzzled Henry Hollins.

Count Alucard shook his head and smiled.

Although the vegetarian vampire knew nothing of the hasty telephone calls that the mayor of Scarcombe had made that morning, he was quick to note that the previous night's happening had not even been given a mention on the front page.

"Never mind, Henry," said the Count, looking down at the cargo boat in the harbour. "The wolves will be far happier where they are going than ever they were in the confines of that compound."

"Are you . . ." Henry hesitated, for he already knew the answer that would follow. "Are you going with them, Count?" he said at last.

"I must, Henry Hollins. I have decided that we belong together, the children of the night and I. Besides, wherever that coffin goes, there go I. It is the only bed I have ever known."

"When do you think you'll be leaving?" asked Henry, in a small, sad voice.

"The boat will sail on tonight's tide," said the Count. "About midnight, I imagine. But as soon as it gets dark, I shall stroll down and smuggle myself aboard. It should not prove too difficult. I shall stow away inside the coffin – nobody will dare to look inside it."

"I wish you didn't have to go *quite* so soon," said Henry. "We've only just met each other again." He paused for a second time, and then added: "It hasn't been much of a holiday for you, has it?"

"No," said Count Alucard, "it has not been a great deal of fun, I must confess. Although I quite enjoyed last night." The Count smiled again. It was a thoughtful smile but Henry detected a twinkle in the vegetarian vampire's dark and usually serious eyes.

"Do you think you might come back again for another holiday?" asked Henry Hollins.

"Who can say? I might. Yes, I might very well return one fine day."

The sun had begun to dip behind their backs and a cool early evening breeze whipped in from across the sea. Count Alucard wrapped his scarlet-lined black cloak firmly round his body and gazed pensively out across the harbour.

164

"If I *do* come back," he continued at last, "I think that next time I shall go to Whitby. Did you know my great-grandfather went there? He spoke very highly of Whitby, did Great-Grandad, according to my father. Yes – next time, it's going to be Whitby or nowhere as far as I'm concerned."

And, having arrived at this decision, Count Alucard lapsed into silence. Henry Hollins did not speak either. There was nothing that needed to be said. They were both content, vampire and boy, to sit side by side at the top of the cliff, each enjoying the other's company, sharing their last few precious minutes together, gazing out at the gently darkening and distant horizon.

"I'm sorry if I seemed rather clumsy," said Barry Barncastle as he escorted his dancing partner off the floor at the Market Hall.

"I'm sure you'll quickly get the hang of it," replied Deborah Padbury with a reassuring smile.

It was the following Wednesday evening and Constable Barncastle had taken his friend's advice, grasped his courage in both hands, and turned up to enlist as a probationer member of the Scarcombe Formation Dancing Team.

"I'm surprised that Norman Woolley isn't here," continued Deborah Padbury, as soon as she was sitting comfortably on one of the gold-painted bamboo chairs which stood all round the dance floor.

"He couldn't come tonight," said Barry Barncastle. "But he'll be here next week, for sure. I do apologise again for treading on your feet a couple of times."

"Don't mention it, Barry," said Deborah Padbury, who had taken off one of her silver-sequined dancing shoes and was gently massaging her big toe. "I thought you did very well for a beginner, all things considered."

This was nothing less than the absolute truth.

Considering that this was his very first attempt at Formation Team Dancing, Barry Barncastle had made more than a reasonable stab at it. Laurence Peasegood's black Spanish-style suit fitted its new owner perfectly. What Barry Barncastle lacked, however, was suitable footwear. It was difficult to dance the *paso doble* in policeman's boots.

Not to worry though, Barry, he told himself, I'll buy a pair of proper patent leather dancing shoes before next Wednesday comes along.

"Would you care for an orange juice, Deborah?" he said aloud. "And shall we also share a packet of coconut macaroons?"

"That's very kind of you, Barry. I'd like that very much," said Deborah Padbury, adding: "You can call me Debbie, if you like."

"Whoopee!" said Barry Barncastle under his breath.

"Fetch, William! Fetch, boy!" cried Norman Woolley, throwing the piece of driftwood as far as he could along the sands.

Norman was to be transferred to the dog-handling branch of the police force, so he decided not to go to the Formation Team's dancing class that evening. Instead, he spent a couple of hours on the moonlit beach, getting to know his new partner in crime prevention.

"Fetch, William! Fetch, Wills! Good boy!" he shouted, trying again.

But although the animal lying full stretch at the policeman's feet wagged its tail energetically, thumping it on the sand, it made no move to retrieve the piece of driftwood. He had not got used to being called "William". Nor did he understand the meaning of "Fetch!"

Less than a week before, when he was the youngest wolf in the compound, the animal answered to the name of "Kevin". On that memorable, if unrecorded, night up on the top of the cliffs, when wolf pack and police dogs had romped together, the zookeepers and policemen who had separated them had not seemed to notice that, when their business was completed, there was one less wolf and one extra police dog.

Taking one thing with another, though, William (a.k.a. Kevin) was quite enjoying his new lifestyle. Admittedly, there were moments when he missed the wolf pack but, on the other hand, he had already made several good friends in the kennels. Also the food was good and, what's more, he quickly adapted to the practice of sleeping with a roof over his head. He enjoyed, too, his close association with this human whom he dragged behind him on a lead and who, for some curious reason, seemed to enjoy throwing pieces of wood and then bringing them back.

"Fetch, William! Come on, Wills, old lad, do your stuff!" entreated Norman Woolley, having retrieved and then despatched again the lump of driftwood for the umpteenth time.

The wolf police dog lowered his head until his lower jaw rested on the sand, pricked up his ears, thwacked his tail down hard again in appreciation, and watched his new companion set out, once more, to bring the driftwood back himself.

"This is the life!" thought William, guessing that if night had come, could supper-time be far away? Oh, yes, indeedy! This was definitely living!

Epilogue

"In the name of the townspeople of Tolokovin, it is my pleasant duty to thank the townspeople of Scarcombe for their most generous gift . . ." Gregori Ilyanovitch, mayor of the little Transylvanian town, paused in his official speech. He was welcoming the wolf pack which had travelled all the way from Scarcombe, first across the Channel aboard the Belgian cargo boat, *La Bernache*, and then across Europe by container lorry.

The mayor stamped his fur-booted feet on the hard snow, pulled his fur hat a little lower over his tingling ears and thumped his gloved hands across his chest, for already the snow had come to Transylvania. What was the point, he asked himself, of making a speech to a pack of caged wolves and a container-lorry driver when not a single solitary member of that number understood a single solitary word of Transylvanian?

It was just after eight p.m. and the townspeople of Tolokovin were where they always were at that time of the evening: sitting in their tiny living rooms, with their doors locked, their windows barred, huddled close to one another, coughing at the smoke which belched from their wood stoves.

No, the time for speech-making would come, Gregori Ilyanovitch decided, weeks from now, when the Tolokovin Town Council entertained the Scarcombe Town Council in the Tolokovin Municipal Hall (the only centrally heated building in the entire town), and with the added benefit of an ample supply of Slopka, the locally fermented drink which ensured that a man could be warm inside if not out.

For the time being, out here on the outskirts of the town, all that was required was a minimum of words and a total lack of ceremony.

"Wolves of Scarcombe, welcome!" declaimed Gregori Ilyanovitch importantly, raising a gloved fist. "Welcome to the forests of Tolokovin! Enjoy your new-found freedom!"

The puzzled wolves scratched at the wooden floors of the cages and sniffed and snuffled and whined at the metal bars. The mayor decided that sufficient words had been said for the occasion. It was almost time to release the wolf pack into the forests.

Gregori Ilyanovitch had been given full assurance that the animals, having spent a lifetime in the close confines of the Wildlife Zoo's compound, were almost tame and would be unlikely to attack a human person. All the same, he decided that it would be better to be safe than sorry. Moving quickly for a man of his portly build he took up a position behind the lorry from where he intended to complete the ceremony. Then, peering nervously round the vehicle, he hand-signalled to the lorry driver to release the wolves.

Pierre Lebrun, the French truck driver, had spent all afternoon constructing an elaborate release device which ensured, when one master cord was pulled from a distance, that all the cage doors would swing upwards simultaneously.

The truck driver tugged hesitantly on the master cord. Nothing happened. He tugged on the cord again, harder this time, and the cage doors flew open in unison. Moving quicker than he had probably ever moved in his life, Pierre Lebrun jumped into the driver's cab. His fingers fumbled as he hastily locked the door. He might just as well have taken his time.

Several seconds elapsed before even the bravest and the boldest of the wolves, Boris himself, ventured out of his cage. Then, putting his nose to the hard-packed snow, he sniffed at the ground beneath, which brought back memories of a native earth he had not sniffed in many a long year.

Lenin was the next to savour freedom, driven by the urge to relieve himself which he proceeded to do, immediately and unceremoniously, on one of the front wheels of the container lorry.

Then the rest of the wolf pack followed: Igor; Ivan; Olga and Dushka; Tracey; Mikhail; Relka . . . one by one, the wolves crept from their cages, cringing and fearful. They herded themselves into a group, all shoving and struggling to get closest to Boris.

Ahead of them lay a vast and seemingly endless forest. They were afraid.

But Boris strove to defy the cowardice of his followers. Leaving the cowering pack behind, he set off across the snow without a backward glance at the cage he had so recently left, or the lorry which had brought him, or even at the warm glow coming from the lights of a myriad oil lamps flickering through the cracks in the shuttered windows of the town at his back.

With his nose still close to the ground, the old wolf padded on, quickening his pace now as he moved through deepening softer snow, towards the shadowy fringe that marked the beginning of the forest.

The wily old wolf sensed he was no longer alone. Curiously, it had been Tracey, the youngest wolf, driven perhaps by the adventurous spirit of youth, who was the first to follow Boris.

Hard on Tracey's heels came the rest. With long, loping strides, the wolf pack caught up with the leader. Then, dogging his paw marks, they raced behind him through the snow into the silence of the forest. They knew that the life which lay ahead of them held a host of hidden surprises, many of which might prove unpleasant. But they were wild and they were free and they were wolves pursuing their birthright.

As they bounded deeper into the tall trees, they were aware of a furry snub-nosed creature with wings like parchment that flitted above their heads.

Some distance behind them, the lorry driver had packed up the cages and was driving off. All that remained on the hard-packed snow was a polished black coffin with a shiny nameplate.

Count Alucard, the vegetarian vampire, knew full well that before the night turned to dawn, he would need to return to human form, and to his resting place. But that could wait. For this moment, he was more than content to zap in and out of the treetops, sometimes wheeling, sometimes diving, but never straying far from the wolf pack roaming below – enjoying, sharing, and rejoicing in the new-won freedom of his four-legged companions – the children of the night.

Other great reads *from* **Red Fox**

Further Red Fox titles that you might enjoy reading are listed
on the following pages. They are available in bookshops or they
can be ordered directly from us.

If you would like to order books, please send this form and
the money due to:

ARROW BOOKS, BOOKSERVICE BY POST, PO BOX 29,
DOUGLAS, ISLE OF MAN, BRITISH ISLES. Please enclose
a cheque or postal order made out to Arrow Books Ltd for the
amount due, plus 75p per book for postage and packing to
a maximum of £7.50, both for orders within the UK. For
customers outside the UK, please allow £1.00 per book.

NAME_____

ADDRESS_____

_____

Please print clearly.

Whilst every effort is made to keep prices low, it is sometimes
necessary to increase cover prices at short notice. If you are
ordering books by post, to save delay it is advisable to phone to
confirm the correct price. The number to ring is THE SALES
DEPARTMENT 071 (if outside London) 973 9700.

Other great reads from **Red Fox**

Enter the gripping world of the REDWALL saga

REDWALL   Brian Jacques

It is the start of the summer of the Late Rose. Redwall Abbey, the peaceful home of a community of mice, slumbers in the warmth of a summer afternoon.

But not for long. Cluny is coming! The evil one-eyed rat warlord is advancing with his battle-scarred mob. And Cluny wants Redwall . . .

ISBN 0 09 951200 9   £3.99

MOSSFLOWER   Brian Jacques

One late autumn evening, Bella of Brockhall snuggled deep in her armchair and told a story . . .

This is the dramatic tale behind the bestselling *Redwall*. It is the gripping account of how Redwall Abbey was founded through the bravery of the legendary mouse Martin and his epic quest for Salmandastron.

ISBN 0 09 955400 3   £3.99

MATTIMEO   Brian Jacques

Slagar the fox is intent on revenge . . .

On bringing death and destruction to the inhabitants of Redwall Abbey, in particular to the fearless warrior mouse Matthias. His cunning and cowardly plan is to steal the Redwall children—and Mattimeo, Matthias' son, is to be the biggest prize of all.

ISBN 0 09 967540 4   £3.99

MARIEL OF REDWALL   Brian Jacques

Brian Jacques starts his second trilogy about Redwall Abbey with the adventures of the mousemaid Mariel, lost and betrayed by Slagar the Fox, but fighting back with all her spirit.

ISBN 0 09 992960 0   £4.50

Other great reads from **Red Fox**

Leap into humour and adventure with Joan Aiken

Joan Aiken writes wild adventure stories laced with comedy and melodrama that have made her one of the best-known writers today. Her James III series, which begins with *The Wolves of Willoughby Chase*, has been recognized as a modern classic. Packed with action from beginning to end, her books are a wild romp through a history that never happened.

THE WOLVES OF WILLOUGHBY CHASE
ISBN 0 09 997250 6   £2.99

BLACK HEARTS IN BATTERSEA
ISBN 0 09 988860 2   £3.50

NIGHT BIRDS ON NANTUCKET
ISBN 0 09 988890 4   £3.50

THE STOLEN LAKE
ISBN 0 09 988840 8   £3.50

THE CUCKOO TREE
ISBN 0 09 988870 X   £3.50

DIDO AND PA
ISBN 0 09 988850 5   £3.50

IS
ISBN 0 09 910921 2   £2.99

THE WHISPERING MOUNTAIN
ISBN 0 09 988830 0   £3.50

MIDNIGHT IS A PLACE
ISBN 0 09 979200 1   £3.50

THE SHADOW GUESTS
ISBN 0 09 988820 3   £2.99

Other great reads from **Red Fox**

Spinechilling stories to read at night

THE CONJUROR'S GAME Catherine Fisher

Alick has unwittingly set something unworldly afoot in Halcombe Great Wood.

ISBN 0 09 985960 2 £2.50

RAVENSGILL William Mayne

What is the dark secret that has held two families apart for so many years?

ISBN 0 09 975270 0 £2.99

EARTHFASTS William Mayne

The bizarre chain of events begins when David and Keith see someone march out of the ground . . .

ISBN 0 09 977600 6 £2.99

A LEGACY OF GHOSTS Colin Dann

Two boys go searching for old Mackie's hoard and find something else . . .

ISBN 0 09 986540 8 £2.99

TUNNEL TERROR

The Channel Tunnel is under threat and only Tom can save it . . .

ISBN 0 09 989030 5 £2.99

Have some supernatural fun with Jonathan's ghost

Dave is just an ordinary schoolboy – except he happens to be a ghost, and only his friend, Jonathan, can see him. With his love of mischief, Dave creates quite a bit of trouble for Jonathan to explain away – but he can also be an extremely useful friend to have when Jonathan's in a fix.

JONATHAN'S GHOST

Jonathan's starting at a new school – but who needs humans when you've got a ghost for a friend?

ISBN 0 09 968850 6 £2.50

SPITFIRE SUMMER

An old wartime ghost seems to be haunting Jonathan – and only Dave can help him.

ISBN 0 09 968850 6 £2.50

THE SCHOOL SPIRIT

A trip to an old mansion brings Jonathan into contact with a triangle of evil determined to find a new victim.

ISBN 0 09 974620 4 £2.50

JONATHAN AND THE SUPERSTAR

Everyone at Jonathan's school thinks Jason Smythe is wonderful – except Dave. Dave senses trouble afoot . . .

ISBN 0 09 995120 7 £2.50

Other great reads from **Red Fox**

Chocks Away with Biggles!

Squadron-Leader James Bigglesworth – better known to his fans as Biggles – has been thrilling millions of readers all over the world with all his amazing adventures for many years. Now Red Fox are proud to have reissued a collection of some of Captain W. E. Johns' most exciting and fast-paced stories about the flying Ace, in brand-new editions, guaranteed to entertain young and old readers alike.

BIGGLES LEARNS TO FLY
ISBN 0 09 999740 1 £3.50

BIGGLES FLIES EAST
ISBN 0 09 993780 8 £3.50

BIGGLES AND THE RESCUE FLIGHT
ISBN 0 09 993860 X £3.50

BIGGLES OF THE FIGHTER SQUADRON
ISBN 0 09 993870 7 £3.50

BIGGLES & CO.
ISBN 0 09 993800 6 £3.50

BIGGLES IN SPAIN
ISBN 0 09 913441 1 £3.50

BIGGLES DEFIES THE SWASTIKA
ISBN 0 09 993790 5 £3.50

BIGGLES IN THE ORIENT
ISBN 0 09 913461 6 £3.50

BIGGLES DEFENDS THE DESERT
ISBN 0 09 993840 5 £3.50

BIGGLES FAILS TO RETURN
ISBN 0 09 993850 2 £3.50

*Other great reads from **Red Fox***

Share the magic of The Magician's House by William Corlett

There is magic in the air from the first moment the three Constant children, William, Mary and Alice arrive at their uncle's house in the Golden Valley. But it's when they meet the Magician, William Tyler, and hear of the Great Task he has for them that the adventures really begin.

THE STEPS UP THE CHIMNEY

Evil threatens Golden House in its hour of need – and the Magician's animals come to the children's aid – but travelling with a fox brings its own dangers.

ISBN 0 09 985370 1   £2.99

THE DOOR IN THE TREE

William, Mary and Alice find a cruel and vicious sport threatening the peace of Golden Valley on their return to this magical place.

ISBN 0 09 997390 1   £2.99

THE TUNNEL BEHIND THE WATERFALL

Evil creatures mass against the children as they attempt to master time travel.

ISBN 0 09 997910 1   £2.99

THE BRIDGE IN THE CLOUDS

With the Magician seriously ill, it's up to the three children to complete the Great Task alone.

ISBN 0 09 918301 9   £2.99

Other great reads *from* **Red Fox**

Discover the wacky world of Spacedog and Roy by Natalie Standiford

Spacedog isn't really a dog at all – he's an alien lifeform from the planet Queekrg, who just happens to *look* like a dog. It's a handy form of disguise – but he's not sure he'll *ever* get used to the food!

SPACEDOG AND ROY

Roy is quite surprised to find an alien spacecraft in his garden – but that's nothing to the surprise he gets when Spacedog climbs out.

ISBN 0 09 983650 5   £2.99

SPACEDOG AND THE PET SHOW

Life becomes unbearable for Spacedog when he's entered for the local pet show and a French poodle falls in love with him.

ISBN 0 09 983660 2   £2.99

SPACEDOG IN TROUBLE

When Spacedog is mistaken for a stray and locked up in the animal santuary, he knows he's in big trouble.

ISBN 0 09 983670 X   £2.99

SPACEDOG THE HERO

When Roy's father goes away he makes Spacedog the family watchdog – but Spacedog is scared of the dark. What can he do?

ISBN 0 09 983680 7   £2.99

Other great reads from **Red Fox**

Giggle and groan with a Red Fox humour book!

Nutty, naughty and quite quite mad, the Red Fox humour list has a range of the silliest titles you're likely to see on a bookshelf! Check out some of our weird and wonderful books and we promise you'll have a ribticklingly good read!

MIAOW! THE CAT JOKE BOOK – Susan Abbott

Be a cool cat and paws here for the purrfect joke! Get your claws into this collection of howlers all about our furry friends that will have you feline like a grinning Cheshire Cat!

ISBN 0 09 998460 1   £1.99

THE SMELLY SOCKS JOKE BOOK – Susan Abbott

Hold your nose . . . here comes the funniest and foulest joke book you're likely to read for a while! Packed with pungent puns and reeking with revolting riddles, this one is guaranteed to leave you gasping for air!

ISBN 0 09 956270 7   £1.99

TUTANKHAMUN IS A BIT OF A MUMMY'S BOY
– Michael Coleman

Have you ever dreaded taking home your school report or a letter from the Head? You're in good company! Did you know that Shakespeare was really "hopeless at English" and that Christopher Columbus had "absolutely no sense of direction"? There's fifty other previously unpublished school reports which reveal hilarious secrets about the famous which not many people know . . .

ISBN 0 09 988180 2   £2.99

THE FISH AND CHIPS JOKE BOOK – Ian Rylett

This book comes complete with a fish-and-chips scratch and sniff panel so you can sniff while you snigger at this delicious collection of piping-hot pottiness! Your tastebuds will be tickled no end with this mouth-watering concoction of tasty gags so tuck into a copy today! It's a feast of fun!

ISBN 0 09 995040 5   £2.99

Other great reads ✦ from Red Fox

Dive into action with Willard Price!

Willard Price is one of the most popular children's authors, with his own style of fast-paced excitement and adventure. His fourteen stories about the two boys Hal and Roger Hunt in their zoo quests for wild animals all contain an enormous amount of fascinating detail, and take the reader all over the world, from one exciting location to the next!

Amazon Adventure
ISBN 0 09 918221 1   £3.50

Gorilla Adventure
ISBN 0 09 918351 X   £3.50

Underwater Adventure
ISBN 0 09 918231 9   £3.50

Lion Adventure
ISBN 0.09 918361 7   £3.50

Volcano Adventure
ISBN 0 09 918241 6   £3.50

African Adventure
ISBN 0 09 918371 4   £3.50

South Sea Adventure
ISBN 0 09 918251 3   £3.50

Diving Adventure
ISBN 0 09 918461 3   £3.50

Arctic Adventure
ISBN 0 09 918321 8   £3.50

Whale Adventure
ISBN 0 09 918471 0   £3.50

Elephant Adventure
ISBN 0 09 918331 5   £3.50

Cannibal Adventure
ISBN 0 09 918481 8   £3.50

Safari Adventure
ISBN 0 09 918341 2   £3.50

Tiger Adventure
ISBN 0 09 918491 5   £3.50

Other great reads ✎ *from* **Red Fox**

Gripping reads by Ruth Thomas

Guilty

Kate is thrilled by the local burglary until playground gossip points the finger at her friend Desmond's father who has recently come out of prison. Kate and Desmond set out together to discover who really is . . . GUILTY!

ISBN 0 09 918519 1   £2.99

The Runaways
Winner of the Guardian Fiction Award

Teachers and parents are suspicious when Julia and Nathan start flashing around the stash of money they found in a deserted house. There's only one way out – to run away . . .

ISBN 0 09 959660 1   £2.99

The New Boy

Donovan is the new boy in the class – secretive, brooding and mysterious. At first Amy is flattered that he wants her to be his friend – until he pushes the limit of her loyalty to the extreme.

ISBN 0 09 973410 9   £2.99

The Secret

When Mum fails to return from her weekend away, Nicky and Roy resolve not to let on to anyone that their mother has abandoned them.

ISBN 0 09 984000 6   £2.99

The Class that Went Wild

Ever since Mrs Lloyd left to have a baby, Class 4L has been impossible! Sean and the gang just get rowdier and rowdier, and even Gillian's twin brother Joseph joins in. Gillian tries to save the situation, but then Joseph goes missing . . .

ISBN 0 09 963210 1   £2.99

Join the RED FOX Reader's Club

The Red Fox Reader's Club is for readers of all ages. All you have to do is ask your local bookseller or librarian for a Red Fox Reader's Club card. As an official Red Fox Reader you only have to borrow or buy eight Red Fox books in order to qualify for your own Red Fox Reader's Clubpack – full of exciting surprises! If you have any difficulty obtaining a Red Fox Reader's Club card please write to: Random House Children's Books Marketing Department, 20 Vauxhall Bridge Road, London SW1V 2SA.